With all of the sincerity and
endearing hope of the original,
Callie of the White Sand
revisits many of the
beloved characters from
Painted Rocks: A Novel,
the debut novel from
Kimberly Ann Freel.

ISBN 0-9619407-9-4

Ask for your copy of *Painted Rocks: A Novel* from your local
bookseller.

Callie
of the
White Sand

By

Kimberly Ann Freel

CMP Publishing Group, LLC
Okanogan, WA

All inquiries, including distributor information, should be addressed to:

CMPPG, LLC
27657 Highway 97
Okanogan, WA 98840

Callie of the White Sand may be ordered from CMPPG, LLC at the above address and at **cmppg.com**

Callie of the White Sand is also available at **Amazon.com**.

email: **cmppg@cmppg.org**
website: **www.cmppg.com**

ISBN13: 978-0-9801554-2-6
Library of Congress Control Number: 2008909192

To my enduring husband, co-parent, and best friend, Christopher. I wouldn't know a thing about romance if it weren't for you.

Prologue

*C*allie bolted awake, suddenly aware that something in the house had changed. It was quiet, almost eerily so. Then someone downstairs began coughing loudly. She let out the breath she had been holding. Clearly it was just her asthmatic older brother getting his nightly drink of water.

She tried to relax and allow sleep back into her mind, but the five-year-old sensed something else was wrong. Jamie was still coughing and it sounded like someone else was too.

There were two bedrooms in the converted attic of their one-hundred-year-old house. She and her three-year-old sister, Libby, shared the northern attic bedroom and her brothers, Jamie and Timothy, seven and nine, shared the southern bedroom. Their parents slept in a bedroom downstairs, at the rear of the house.

The house was a wonder, a maze of steep staircases to the attic and basement and charming, high-ceilinged rooms surrounding a large, central kitchen. It was completed on the outside by a wraparound porch with spindled railing and a proud, steep roofline. The eaves made the attic walls slanted, giving their rooms a cozy feel. Their parents dreamed of someday restoring the historic house to its original glory.

Callie loved it as much as they did. She spent many nights in her room, sitting at their wide, multi-paned bedroom window, reveling in the silk-padded window seat, dressed up in her grandmother's old clothes, and pretending that it was the "olden days" and the house was brand new and she was its lady.

Now, though, she thought the normal yellow cast by her moon-shaped nightlight looked eerily orange. The air tasted of the time Timothy had made her try to eat his dirty sock. Thinking of it made her sick to her stomach. Perhaps she needed a drink of water too.

Careful not to disturb Libby, she slipped from her bed, her calico nightgown sweeping the floor. She padded to the closed door and swung it open. A sea of white fog greeted her, curling around her ankles, obscuring the oak floors beneath it. The floor felt hot, which was odd, because normally the cold of the wooden floors compelled her to fairly sail across them, seeking the braided rug at the top of the stairs.

It was with a deep breath and the coughing that ensued, that Callie realized what the white fog was. It was smoke! Mrs. Stokes had talked about house fires in their Kindergarten class. They had talked about what to do if they had one in their own home. Was that what was happening here?

Callie could hear her sister begin to cough in the room behind her. She closed the door so that the smoke wouldn't continue to choke Libby. Stifling her own coughs, with tears beginning to stream down her face, Callie tried hard to conquer the sudden fear that was overcoming her with every step. She needed to save her brothers and her sister. She summoned all of the bravery a five-year-old possessed.

Callie ran the remaining fifteen steps to her brothers' room. She wasted a minute with knocking and then she realized that they might be asleep and that she needed to rouse them more forcefully. She flung open the door. Through the thick haze of smoke, she could see that Jamie's bed was empty. It must have been his coughing that she'd heard downstairs.

Timothy was asleep, but coughing that same irritated cough that she felt torturing her throat.

He was groggy as she roused him. She shook him and then finally, yelled at him that he needed to come with her. There was a fire!

Timothy awoke fully at the mention of fire and his instincts as Callie's older brother took over. He led her quickly back to her room and scooped up tiny Libby in his own arms. He took them both past the hallway bathroom to the top of the staircase.

What greeted them there was the most horrific scene that Callie would ever recall. The stairs were afire, the flames licking at the low, shag carpet and sending more blackened smoke their way. The house had begun to groan under the duress of fire and it was clear that their way out was completely impassable. Timothy quickly reversed his path to the girls' bedroom. He called for Callie, but she stood, mesmerized by the crawling purple and red flames. They seemed to whisper to her. What were they saying?

A sudden blast of hot air through the staircase blew her black hair off her shoulders and startled Callie into running back to her room.

Timothy was working on the window. An unfortunate byproduct of living in an old house was that the window casings had many layers of paint. They had never opened the bedroom window and now it was apparent that the reason they hadn't was that it was painted shut. Timothy was using the full capacity of his nine-year-old brain when he threw Callie's wooden stool through it, intent on bringing fresh air to their suffering lungs and on finding a way to escape.

His only mistake had been choosing the girls' room as their escape route. The wraparound porch roof extended around the Southern and Western sides of the house. The boys had a clear view of the roofline below them and they had often pondered whether they could get out of the house this way.

Timothy realized his mistake, and cleared away the cloth he'd put under the door so that they could all run back across the hallway to the other room. He opened the door to a blast of heat. The fire had spread to the upstairs hallway. There would be no way across now.

He and Callie quickly closed the door to the fire, which was now roaring menacingly closer to their location. They replaced the bedclothes under the door and, with Libby in tow, took themselves over to the window seat, where they commenced to screaming out the window and taking in gulps of fresh air.

The nearest neighbors, though, were more than half a block away. Their nice big house had come with an expansive lawn and a border of beautiful poplar trees blocking the wind from the North. They couldn't be seen or heard from where they were.

Callie prayed that their parents would be able to rescue them. Why hadn't they ever gotten a ladder to get out of their room, like their teacher had talked about?

It seemed like hours, though it really was only minutes before the three of them began to succumb to smoke inhalation. The open window only seemed to attract more smoke from below and their little lungs couldn't take the onslaught.

Callie felt consciousness slipping away, which was merciful, because the floor on which they sat was burning through also. Her perch at the edge of the window seat became an opening into the fire's abyss, but she was barely conscious of the slow singing of her arm and torso. She let out an unconscious sigh of pain as the right side of her face became unbearably hot.

She saw a light in the distance. Could it be a fireman coming finally to rescue all of them? She tried to move toward the light, but it seemed more rapidly to be moving toward her. She reached for it.

Then she was snatched away, cruelly, the cold air of the fall night hitting her seared skin, creating a fog of pain like she'd never felt. Glove-shod hands handled her small body lightly, but quickly. She was put into an ambulance. There were now lights everywhere. Was she alive?

She slipped into the arms of oblivion as the ambulance crew tried fervently to save her fire-ravaged little soul. They would have their work cut out for them, for Callie's battle was only just beginning.

The arsonist had watched as the flames licked the curtains inside the window. The propane torch did its job nicely in lighting the front door and doorframe. Then he noticed the kitchen window, open just a crack. Still, he was pretty sure by the peeling paint and absence of vehicles outside the house, that the home was empty. He threw the blowtorch inside the open window. 'That's enough for now,' he thought. 'Time to become an observer.'

He looked around again for signs of occupancy. No family car out front. No bicycles leaning against the front porch railing. No barbecue on the porch. Still, there was a garage out back and he'd had no luck getting in. He had thought about torching the garage. Flames were flames and he got a rush no matter what, but he had taken one look at the stately, ancient Victorian on a Sunday drive weeks ago and, since, he had longed to see it encased in an inferno, flames licking the gingerbread trim, defining each carved rail on the wraparound porch. He had imagined it would be gorgeous—the hottest parts of the flame glowing fuschia and indigo, warming even his frigid core, if only for a few precious moments.

So he went for the house. He got back to the truck. Everything was just as he had left it in the cab. Time to go for a drive, find the fire station, wait for the call to come and watch the volunteer firefighters rush about. Time to follow them, at a safe and sure distance.

The Victorian was just as he had imagined it, every careful detail of the porch alight as the flames licked across it. Lattice lit in a criss-cross pattern, the edges glowing orange as fuel met fire. He let the blaze dance in his eyes from the seat of the truck, then he nonchalantly made his way among horrified neighbors. People gathered around fires like bees to honey. He found he could always blend among spectators. Only these people weren't exclaiming over the terrific beauty of a wasted, abandoned structure. They were talking about the 'Jones' family. Somebody lived here. It was then that the screams registered in his buzz-addled brain. It sounded like children. It sounded as if they were dying. He blanched.

He'd made a mistake.

Chapter 1

*Jamie and Timothy often came to her at night,
all full of mischief, their eyes dancing with tales of
train robbery and bounty hunting, like they'd seen on
Dad's western TV shows. They had big plans when
they grew up and they would most definitely be the
bad guys, because outlaws seemed to have the most
fun.*

*Timothy, though, being the oldest would
inevitably reason that they were unlikely to find a
train to rob nowadays. The commercial railway
didn't really carry rich people much. If people had
money, they traveled by private airplane. And if
Timothy, Jamie, and Callie bounty-hunted, they
would essentially be chasing themselves, since they
wanted to be outlaws.*

*There wasn't time for big plans in the wee hours
of the night anyway. They would have to settle for
a smaller brand of tomfoolery. What if they booby-
trapped the stairway so that Mom's heart would get
to thumping good when she came to get them up in
the morning? That could be accomplished. Jamie,
Timothy, and Callie put their heads together while
Libby slept. No sense waking the baby.*

*They had the whole thing rigged so that when
Mom stepped on the fifth step, the fishing line that
they poised just an inch above the tread would
initiate a chain reaction that would ultimately bring*

her face to face with Callie's sock monkey. Only the monkey wasn't wearing his usual face. For good measure, Jamie put his vampire mask over the monkey's head. That ought to give her a good, first-thing-in-the-morning rush!

The boys' room was slightly closer to the staircase than the girls', so they decided to wait out the morning in the hallway outside the boys' door. They would doze, but just for while, until nearer to the target time. They wouldn't want to miss the expression on Mom's face.

Callie thought she could hold out until morning, watching her brothers sleep, keeping her eyes open so that she could be the hero and wake them up when she heard the customary toilet flush that signaled her mother's early rise. But, her eyes would sink, despite her every attempt to prop them open. And her brothers would vanish again, just as they had seventeen years before in a haze of smoke and pain.

*C*allie woke up in her hut, the mosquito netting swaying in the early morning breeze, the tangy, salty air assailing her nostrils, the fresh morning sun beckoning her to her daily ritual—an early walk on the white-sand beach. She felt as she always did when she lost sight of her peaceful, sleeping brothers—bereft, and tired, always so tired, as if she really stayed up rigging the staircase.

Too sad, too spent to cry, again, for Jamie and Timothy and Libby and their parents, Callie moved silently through her morning routine. She sliced papaya, bought from the market the day before, appreciating the luscious fruit as it satiated her hunger and reminded her how very far she was away from the real world. She poured a glass of bottled water and washed down her morning toothpaste and her medication.

After a mild painkiller took effect, she stretched

away the stiffness that the scars bound into the surface of her skin.

She stepped to the doorway and took in the beauty of the sunlit beach and the cerulean blue water that slipped quietly to and fro on the shore. She traveled barefoot on the silky white sand, feeling its morning coolness in contrast to the tropical sun. Since she was on the leeward side of the island, she could walk a short distance to a point where the beach was gated off outside the shipbuilders' marina. The rest of the walk was open to her enjoyment. The white-crowned pigeons kept her company. Other than that, she had complete solitude.

Callie came to Belize six months ago. She came as a volunteer for the home health clinic run by the country's only hospital. It was a bid to end her isolation in the States, to venture out among new people who didn't know about her past or about her scars. She had worked in home health care in the Seattle area for a time after finishing high school; but inevitably, the people she worked with would figure out who she was and what she had done.

Belize City would afford her obscurity, she thought. She didn't need to work and she could have just quit working altogether, but Callie had spent most of her life between the ages of five and fifteen completely left to her own devices. She wanted to be around people, and the idea of working with poverty-stricken elders and children in the remote country of Belize appealed to her sense of charity.

Callie didn't quite anticipate the animosity most traditional Belizeans felt for young, attractive American women. She was ogled regularly by the men and repeatedly rejected by the women because their society believed American women were promiscuous and untrustworthy.

The other home-health aides at the clinic refused

to befriend her with her pale skin and dignified manner. They were suspicious of her and her intentions. The doctor overseeing the clinic thought Callie interesting, indeed. He was the first to discover her scars. Callie was careful to wear long, full, loose clothing to stay cool and to protect the scars on her arm and torso, which weren't entirely surgically corrected. They needed to be kept from the sunlight.

In her third week at the clinic, the doctor found her in the storage area consolidating medications from free samples that had been shipped. She was opening small bottles of diabetes medication and pouring them into a larger bottle, which would last a month for each patient. He came behind her and rested his hands on her shoulders, his groin planted firmly against her buttocks.

"You can let the nurses do that work, Callie. I can think of more important things for you to do."

She'd closed her eyes and remained silent, trying to will him away from her before the others noticed his attention.

"Beautiful Callie. I need to go to the Madison Hotel to meet a visiting colleague. Won't you join me? I'm sure he would be impressed by you."

"I told Ismelda that I would finish up this shipment so we could get rid of some of the bigger boxes. They're cluttering the storage room." Still, she did not face him, but tried in vain to step away from the heat of his arousal. He stank of sour rum and body odor. The bile rose in her throat.

"I just sent Ismelda to check blood pressures at the Mission. She won't be back before the end of the day."

"I'm sure, Doctor, that she would know if I neglected the duties she assigned me for the day."

"I'll talk to her," he assured her, his breath brushing her ear as he lowered his hands from her shoulders and ran them up and down her arms.

Callie cringed even now, as her skin crawled, remembering the shame of that day. She kept her steps steady as she flushed again with mortification that the middle-aged doctor, upon feeling the uneven skin on her arm, turned her quickly and ripped open her gauzy blouse. What she recognized in his eyes as filthy arousal changed immediately to horror and then to regret. As Callie watched the emotions assail his face, she reacted quickly by pulling her blouse shut with one hand and slapping him with the other.

Callie never went back to the clinic, but she had no family in the States anymore. She wasn't ready to go home, wherever that was. The Belizean Cayes offered her solitude while she figured out what she was going to do. She chartered a boat to Caye Caulker, a remote island with low-key tourism and private, friendly natives; and she rented a bungalow on the beach. The island natives may have gossiped about the white girl, but they all kept a polite distance. As long as she followed their carefully laid rules about island conservation, she was welcome.

Her short retreat extended to a month-long stay and now she wasn't sure she would ever go back to the States again. She took to journaling and going for short swims and walks when she felt restless. People had caused Callie nothing but trouble and she wasn't sure she had been so smart to feel that she needed to be among them.

She was anchorless, shifting through life like a buoy without a chain. Callie was intelligent and creative, but her attention span had been altered by her traumatic childhood and surgeries too numerous to count. She dreamed of a job that could finally channel her artistic energies. She didn't so much want to be alone, but to surround herself with intimate friends who knew about her past, but didn't judge her by it. Did she want love, romance? Well, who didn't want to be loved?

Callie pondered her solitude once again, her feet kicking up sand, her eyes on the clouds of an approaching tropical storm, when her lack of attention sent her sprawling into the arms of a man who had laid himself on the windward side of a tuft of sand and grass. Callie's beach had been invaded and her distraction had just gotten the best of her.

Chapter 2

Strong arms embraced Callie, keeping her from falling face-first into the sand. He smelled of plumeria, bougainvillea flowers, and coconut oil. Callie noticed as she placed her hands on his chest to rise that it was bronze and bare, except for the lei around his neck. She jumped to her feet almost as quickly as she went down.

Mortified at her clumsiness, Callie could barely look the stranger in the face.

"I'm sorry," she mumbled, averting her eyes. "I wasn't watching where I was walking."

By now, the stranger was on his feet as well. "Are you okay? I didn't realize my section of the beach had a path through it!"

He maneuvered his body between Callie and the morning sun and then he caught her intriguing green eyes.

His eyes were the blue of the Caribbean Sea. Callie couldn't help but stare back at this chestnut-haired sun god. She brushed the sand from her cotton pants, still caught in his gaze. Callie was tall and it was rare that she met a man that she didn't look levelly in the eye. At least six feet plus, this man was all muscle and masculinity, except for the flowers he wore in his lei and on his swim trunks. He made the lanky Callie feel petite.

"I'm really sorry," Callie repeated. "I've been walking here everyday for months. I thought this bungalow was still empty."

"Oh I just flew in this morning. Friendly place. I thought only Hawaiians greeted their guests with leis and beautiful beach maidens."

An oversized grin spread across his tanned face as he sought her smile in return.

Callie was unused to close male attention. She'd spent most of the last five years with her face in a state of slow repair. She had only recently stopped taking the steroids that made her face puffy and kept her from rejecting her skin grafts. She felt good enough about her facial scars to finally tuck her straight, shoulder-length hair behind her ear instead of wearing it over her right eye and cheek. The frank examination this man was making of her made her intensely uncomfortable.

Callie couldn't find a smile in return. She looked for an escape route. "I, um, need to be getting back. I have a date for breakfast," Callie lied.

"That's unfortunate. I had hoped you were traveling solo, like me. I'd like to talk to you some more sometime, since we've already shared a patch of white sand," he smiled charmingly.

"Maybe I'll see you again sometime," Callie lied again, knowing that she would not walk this direction again as long as the stranger occupied this bungalow.

"I'm Jake, by the way. Jake Lamb." He held out his hand in greeting.

Callie reluctantly took his hand, her slender fingers enveloped in his strong grip. She flushed at the renewed contact.

"Callie."

"Well, Callie of the White Sand, it's been a pleasure seeing you this morning." He smiled that engaging smile again.

This time, Callie smiled back. After all, he'd been nothing short of charming and she wouldn't see him again, if she could help it.

His breath caught as her smile transformed her once-sullen face. She was a beauty—milky white skin with a flush to her cheeks, contrasting with her jet black hair and cat-like eyes rimmed by soft black lashes.

Jake was determined to see her again.

As it turned out, the island of Caye Caulker was way too small to avoid a man as imposing as Jake Lamb. Callie ran into him, less physically this time, at the market where she shopped for fresh fish for supper.

She reached for a small package of filleted tuna and heard his familiar timbre.

"That certainly doesn't look like it would feed more than one person. Why, even you could starve eating just that tiny morsel."

Callie looked to her left to find Jake fingering a packaged whole swordfish.

"What were you planning to do with that? Feed half of the island?"

Jake feigned injury at her sarcastic words. "There's a refrigerator at the bungalow. I could have leftovers, for weeks…"

Callie laughed at that. She had a musical lilt to her laugh. It sounded like the joyful tinkle of chimes to Jake. He could get used to amusing Callie.

"Seriously, Callie of the White Sand, do you plan to dine alone on that meager tuna this evening, or could I convince you to join me for supper at *Levinger's*?"

So he'd already figured out the nicest restaurant on the island, Callie thought. If he was planning to eat there regularly, then he must have a large budget. It wasn't like she was hurting financially either, but Callie, by nature, was conservative about money.

"I couldn't possibly impose on your dinner plans, Jake. Besides, I'm not dressed," Callie looked down at her coral caftan and her navy espadrilles.

Jake did have to agree that her choice of clothing was hardly flattering to her willowy figure, nor was it fancy enough for the restaurant on the point; but he had to get her to agree to go out with him sometime.

"You don't have plans, then, with, um, anybody?"

Callie decided to be truthful this time. "No, I don't have dinner plans, other than grilling this tasty piece of tuna."

"Could you save it for lunch tomorrow? We could swing by your bungalow in my golf cart and you could change. I would love the company."

Jake's clear blue eyes and sincerity pierced Callie's lonely reserve. What could it hurt? After all, he was obviously just vacationing here. He'd be gone in a week, two at the most. Then, after that, her quiet island existence could return to normal.

"Okay, then I guess you have a date," she replied, smiling shyly as Jake helped carry her shopping basket to the front counter.

The clerk turned curious eyes to both of them as he realized that one of the tourists had just picked up his regular, but mysterious customer. He was a handsome fellow and American, which made him a good match for the young lady. He wouldn't want a local picking up on her, for she really was a stranger to the Caye. Locals and visitors did not often mix well. Of course, tourists rarely stayed as long as this one.

Callie thanked the weathered Garafunan clerk politely. The younger man gave him a conspiratorial wink as they left the market. The clerk shook his head in amazement. This particular young woman had been the most steadfast loner he'd observed in awhile. The strapping American must have really laid on the charm. He chuckled softly and returned to washing the windows at the storefront as Jake and Callie got into Jake's red golfcart and drove away, her canvas shopping bag perched casually in the back as if it belonged there.

*A*t Callie's bungalow, she exchanged her frumpy caftan for a slim, longsleeved, canary yellow tunic and a white gauze, calf-length skirt. She put a silver-toned braided belt low around her waist and pulled the top half of her hair into an abalone and silver clasp.

Callie was a minimalist when it came to makeup, because her repaired skin was particularly sensitive to beauty products. She put a glaze of cinnamon-colored gloss onto her lips and a flash of mascara onto her upper lashes. Then she examined herself seriously in the mirror. Excitement flushed her face. Her appearance matched the nerves she felt inside.

Callie had never allowed more than just a casual date. She'd attracted unfamiliar attention since surgery had transformed her appearance and she was still unsure how this translated into accepting male company. Jake would be no different, she knew, because when it came down to him wanting to snorkel or frolic on a pier with her, he would never understand her reticence to do so. She didn't wear a bathing suit, but a wetsuit top, because she couldn't expose her skin to the harsh tropical sunlight, nor was she willing to reveal the secrets that her scarred arms would inevitably expose.

She was undeniably apprehensive about having a dinner date. She knew Jake would be an amusing companion. She would just have to deal with him later when he asked for more than she was willing to give. Callie grabbed a beaded handbag and threw her gloss, her identification, and a small amount of cash inside and left her bungalow to join her date.

Chapter 3

*W*hat surprised Callie most about her supper with Jake had nothing to do with the gorgeous ocean view from *Levinger's* dining windows or the delectable gourmet cuisine. It was his gentle, guiding hand on the small of her back as he ushered her through the outer door, his invitation to seat her before he took his own seat, and Jake's polite consideration of the wait staff that most pleased Callie. Jake was a gentleman and Callie knew this was a rare find in her generation of men.

Though Jake was probably at least five years her senior, she expected him to be less chivalrous, more like the crass, aloof young men she'd known from years spent in a group home. Her dad, her *real* dad, had been unfailingly polite and gentle. He had held open doors for his "girls," taught his sons never to 'beat-up' on their younger sisters, and she had never seen him raise his voice or his hand to her mother. Callie had thought those qualities were lost to men her age.

Her dad had also been a large man—that was where she had gotten her height. The memories of her father were distant, but warm, and she wondered if Jake Lamb had won her attention because of a faint resemblance to Barron Jones.

Jake read her thoughts. "You keep looking at me as though I remind you of somebody."

"You do. I was just thinking that you look a little like my father."

"That's good, I hope."

"You know, I'm not sure, because I don't remember him very well. I lost my family when I was only five."

"That's horrible. Why?"

Callie was uncomfortable with this part of her history, for the sheer fact that she remembered little and it pained her to recall so little of the family she missed so much.

"It was a terrible accident. Anyway, they didn't raise me. My adoptive father was nothing like you. He was a doctor."

Jake snorted politely. Callie didn't know if this was sarcasm or encouragement, so she continued.

"I was adopted after I lost my family by Cyrus and Constance Justice. He was a psychiatrist. She was a counselor. Our relationship was not ideal. I'm sure they never really wanted a child. I know they never want to see me again." Realizing that she was rambling, Callie abruptly stopped, took a sip of her wine and regarded Jake warily.

He didn't respond.

"Can we talk about something else?" She shifted uncomfortably. "How much do you know about the Belizean Cayes?"

They held casual conversation for the remainder of dinner, discussing the many conservation efforts the Belizeans were implementing to save their mangroves, salt-water crocodiles, and rare species of birds. They talked about weather and travel.

Over dessert, Jake asked Callie if she liked to snorkel. Belize boasted the second longest barrier reef in the world and he planned to rent a boat and skipper to take him out to the reef the next morning. Would she like to go?

This was precisely the question that Callie dreaded. She never learned to snorkel and it made her nervous to do so, though she heard that salt-water snorkeling provided some buoyancy, and of course, there were other reasons as well.

"It's very sweet of you to ask, Jake, but I have plans for tomorrow."

"Oh, well, that's too bad," Jake tried to hide his disappointment. He truly enjoyed Callie's company. She was intelligent and unafraid to show it and she didn't ask him tons of questions, something that always turned him off. He sensed that she was as private as he. It lent her an aura of mystery.

Callie realized that Jake wasn't going to ask her what her plans were. She felt bad for disappointing him, so she volunteered just a morsel.

"I'm planning to spend the day photographing some of the foliage of the island at the forest reserve. I've been journaling and I'd like to add some pictorial information to my writing."

"Are you planning to have your work published when you leave?"

"To be truthful, I haven't really thought about it."

"You know a lot about this little country and even more about the Cayes. I'm sure what you've written would be interesting to tourists like myself."

Callie had written about the Cayes and Belizean history in her journal, but she'd also spent a great deal of time working out her traumatic past on paper. There was no better therapy, as far as she was concerned. It was true she wanted to add pictures, but she knew she would never publish all of her journal work.

"I'm flattered, Jake, really. But this is more of a hobby for me."

"Could I possibly join you at the reserve?" Jake held his breath and hoped Callie would not think him presumptuous.

"I wouldn't want you to miss your snorkeling trip.

The rain we had earlier today is supposed to pass. I've heard tomorrow will be gorgeous weather."

"I could postpone my charter for a day if you will allow me to join you."

Callie didn't see the harm in it. It would be a pleasure to share the island with another person for a change.

"I suppose that would be fine," she offered.

"Maybe you can join me on the reef some other day."

"Yes, maybe." Callie finished her coconut crème broule and washed it down with the house coffee, a Columbian blend that had a distinct hint of nutmeg. She wanted to show her appreciation to Jake for the dinner and for his good company.

"I've really enjoyed dining with you, Jake. Maybe we could do it again while you're here—my treat next time."

Jake took Callie home to her bungalow. He stole glances as she glowed ethereal in the balmy, moonlit night. He walked her to her door with his hand on the small of her back once more. His touch was hesitant, but somehow familiar.

"Callie, I'm looking forward to tomorrow. Should I meet you here?"

"I'll be ready at ten."

"Will I see you on the beach earlier?" He raised his eyebrows suggestively.

She laughed. "Nope. I'm going to save my energy for the littoral forest. You should too. When I take a hike, I'm serious about it."

"I'll remember that.

"Callie?" Jake was suddenly serious.

"Yes, Jake?"

"When you talked about your family earlier, I didn't mean to act as if I didn't care. My family history isn't exactly simple either."

"Really? You seem so well-adjusted."

He laughed then, with the polite little snort that Callie was coming to recognize as ironic.

"You obviously need to get to know me better."

"I hope to," she said tentatively.

"Then I'll see you in the morning," Jake winked, exuding charm once again.

"Goodnight, Jake." Callie's voice was barely audible and her eyes were luminous, child-like. He wanted to kiss her, but he thought better of it. She slipped into her bungalow and slid the door closed.

*B*elize was among the few Caribbean nations who had the foresight to preserve its native mangroves, despite an increasing demand for sandy beaches. The littoral forest was a sanctuary to mangroves and almost one hundred rare species of birds. Ignoring the onslaught of insects, hatchlings glorying from the previous day's rain, Callie and Jake explored the Northern tip of the island. Callie pointed out an osprey nest and photographed a rufus-necked rail, a bird rarely seen elsewhere in the world.

Jake's skin crawled when Callie pointed to a dank lagoon and he saw what she was gesturing at: a salt-water crocodile the size of a canoe. He was all for nature, but Jake insisted that they emerge from the fog of insects to eat their lunch on the beach.

All the while, Jake marveled at Callie's knowledge about the tiny island of Caye Caulker. She spoke of ecology, geography, and environmental conservation as if she was well-educated in the subject.

"How have you learned all of this, Callie? You amaze me."

"I've observed a lot. I don't frequently hang

around people here, because I prefer the quiet, but I have befriended an American guide who has lived here for twenty years and he taught me a lot of what I've passed on to you. I don't read well, so I've had to ask questions."

"You're not a reader? I can't say I read much for enjoyment, but books are necessary to my work. It surprises me that you don't read since you're a writer and because you're so knowledgeable."

"I've had trouble concentrating, ever since I was a kid. My adopted parents tucked me away from the world and the only company I had was that of my governess and the television. Mrs. Wembly would bring me these big, fat books to try and lure me away from the T.V.. I would always lose focus after about a chapter, so I'd put the book down and make up my own ending. Even when I had the option to go to school, teachers didn't take well to my altered versions of classic stories. I gave up trying to be a reader and I didn't go to college at all. I can make up a good story, though, and journaling is therapeutic. So I write in short vignettes. It works for me."

"I would love to read your journals sometime," Jake said in earnest.

Callie withdrew. The contents of her journals were sacred and sharing them would be tantamount to telling Jake everything about her past. She couldn't stand for the abuse and the neglect of her early childhood to be laid bare like that. It was painful enough to recall, without making it subject to any kind of scrutiny.

"You would find them completely boring," she said. "I'm really not educated or descriptive enough to make them worth reading."

Jake looked into Callie's eyes and she averted her gaze. He tucked a finger under her chin and pulled her attention back to him. "Everything about you is interesting, Callie. You're anything but boring."

Callie flushed and rose, brushing sandwich crumbs from her khaki pants. She looked to the sky in time to see a plane coming in for a landing at the airstrip. "Looks like more people are joining us on our island adventure."

"Well they'll never find a tour guide as informative as you," Jake complimented and followed Callie's lead.

Callie showed Jake around the whole island. She spent the afternoon giving him a detailed tour afoot, at first, and then from his golf cart as their legs grew tired.

Jake offered to take Callie to dinner once again and she insisted on taking him to the local tavern for fish and chips instead. They each drank a Guinness and gorged themselves on freshly-caught, battered fish.

They were quiet during their ride home. The sun set early this close to the equator, but the moon and copious stars lit their journey, the tangy tropical air settling over them. Jake stopped his golf cart several yards shy of Callie's door, wanting to walk her back to her bungalow.

They joined hands when he helped her out of the cart, and neither of them broke the contact. As they approached her door, Jake turned to Callie and grasped her other hand. She was breathtaking in the moonlight, her raven hair shimmering blue. Her creamy skin looked as if it was lit from within.

Jake was like a twilight god, his chestnut hair curled casually over his brow and his striking blue eyes deepening with the darkness. He looked into her eyes, so serious, so utterly irresistible. Callie felt an unfamiliar warmth creep through her veins. She suddenly wanted this man beyond reason, inhibitions be damned.

Jake sensed Callie's need as surely as he felt his own. He dropped her hands only long enough to put his slender hands gently about her neck, the tips of his thumbs tracing her lovely jaw. Then he leaned in and ever so gently kissed Callie's parted lips, deepening his embrace gradually, groaning softly deep in his throat as he tasted the depths of her mouth.

Jake dropped his hands from beneath her silky hair to her lower back, pressing her hips into his, drawing a sigh of surprise from Callie. He tasted her lemon and vinegar flavor, repeatedly touching his hot tongue to the tip of hers. She invited more, matching his enthusiasm with her own.

Then Jake touched her shoulders and began to rub her upper arms. Callie tensed and quickly pulled away, cruelly ending what had been the sweetest embrace of Jake Lamb's life. He was disappointed by her withdrawal, but there had been something else. He had expected skin as smooth and beautiful beneath her tunic as he'd felt beneath her hair and jaw. Her arms hadn't felt that way. He quickly dismissed the thought—it was probably just the fabric of her long-sleeved shirt.

Callie, though, was devastated by her knee-jerk reaction to the contact. She didn't know just where she had intended to stop her romantic embrace with Jake, but she was quite sure by the look in his eyes that her reaction had just hurt him terribly by withdrawing so abruptly.

"Jake, I…" Callie began.

"Shhh, Callie, don't apologize. I came on too strong. I'm not usually so forward on a second date." Jake acted casual, though his emotions still ran high.

Callie was embarrassed at her own wantonness. She tried a lighter tone as she said, "It wasn't exactly our second date. After all, I did take a tumble in the sand with you yesterday."

Jake smiled and took Callie's cue, "That is true. We've hardly done anything tonight that would outweigh that first roll we took together!"

"I'm going to have to walk that section of the beach again tomorrow, aren't I?"

"Oh, Callie, I wish you would," Jake countered. "I want to see you again. Can we meet in the afternoon at the *Playa Bistro*, say two o'clock?"

"Let's do that, Jake. Until then, I'm going to turn in. A good book awaits."

"As long as it's only a book and not some other lustful suitor, then I shall take my leave also."

Callie suddenly turned serious again, giving Jake his first insight into her reclusive existence, "No, Jake. There has never been anyone else. I can't explain, just know that another man is not the issue."

She looked forlorn as she opened her bungalow door and bid him goodnight, flipped on her overhead light, and closed the door softly behind her.

Jake wanted to follow her, to find out what her words meant, to unfold the mystery that was Callie. He didn't even know her last name.

Jake knew one thing for sure—he came to Belize for a much-needed vacation, instead he had gotten into a situation he hadn't bargained for. Women had been throwing themselves at Jake's feet since he'd filled out his size fourteens at the ripe age of sixteen. He had fun with many of them. Feminine company was both familiar and welcome in the limited social time he had outside of work.

Callie gripped him far deeper than any of those women and he'd known her barely two days. She was obviously independent, gorgeous, and clever; but, there was vulnerability beneath that he couldn't lay his finger on. And that kiss, well that was something he was sure would interrupt his sleep for many nights to come. Unless, he could convince her to join him in his bed sometime, he thought devilishly.

He drove home in the peaceful, tropical night. It seemed like their entire section of the Caye had already settled in. Jake decided he was going to enjoy his

Belizean vacation very much.

Callie was in complete turmoil. On the one hand, their evening together was lovely. Her whole day, really, had been dominated by handsome, funny Jake Lamb. He was a total gentleman. He was sweet and his kiss, oh boy, it had been both soft and demanding, and mind-boggling.

On the other hand, she didn't know him, really, at all. With very little effort, he had invaded her peaceful island existence. Callie didn't like it, whatsoever, having to explain herself to anybody, let alone a man who wouldn't leave her alone. He was disruptive. He was gorgeous. She sighed again.

Jake hadn't really demanded anything of her. In fact, he was nothing short of encouraging and patient when she made excuses for not snorkeling the next day.

Suddenly Callie was exhausted, too spent to read anything, too unsure of her own feelings regarding Jake Lamb. She would deal with it all in the morning.

Never given to tears, because she'd cried too much already in her short life, Callie, nevertheless cried herself to sleep that night in her bungalow, because she was alone again, and she feared she would never be strong enough to change that.

Chapter 4

*J*ake caught an eight o'clock charter taking him about a mile westward to the Belizean Barrier Reef. Between sun and surf, he spent a glorious morning snorkeling with numerous colorful fish including parrot fish and barracuda alike. The reef was awash with color—purples, reds, and yellows set on a backdrop of incredibly clear cerulean blue. Each alcove he explored was new and intricate. The anemones waved, the sponges contracted. The tropical fish peeked coyly from crevices.

He took underwater pictures with a plastic-covered disposable camera. He smiled as he thought of Callie and how much she would enjoy the photos once he had them developed.

She too would be taking pictures and journaling all day. Maybe they could have an intimate evening at his condo after their bistro lunch. He could take his camera to the one-hour-photo while they ate. Then they could share their evening over photos of glorious Belize.

Jake was a moderately accomplished cook. Perhaps she'd let him have a go at her fillet of tuna. He doubted it, but he was mulling over other menu options as he explored the gorgeous reef. Maybe it was all of the salt water he swallowed, but he had a craving for seafood, maybe shrimp and calamari in a light garlic sauce.

He decided to ask the captain. "I'd like to cook dinner tonight. What's the best catch of the day on this

Caye, Captain?"

The captain was native Belizean and he spoke mostly in a Caribbean version of Creole, but he toned it down for his visitor. "Lobster. We got de best and jou buy right from de pier, off'n de boat. Delicious." He smacked his lips for emphasis.

"Jou got a date, Dr. Jake?" He smiled conspiringly. He knew that the young man was a doctor on vacation. An American doctor deserved special treatment, so he took him to only the best parts of the reef.

"I hope so. I met a girl and she took me on a tour of the island. She knows quite a bit about Caye Caulker, maybe even as much as a native."

"No, dat not possible." The captain shook his head. "She may know de island, but she never know de heart. We keep that'n close and don' share wit' de visitors."

Jake smiled. He enjoyed the captain's candor. Being in Belize was such a departure from his fast-paced life at home. It was rural, more like the places where he grew up. He felt totally relaxed, a million miles away from the melee of his job, a job he loved but felt frequently drained by. This was exactly what he needed.

Maybe that's why he felt so immediately attracted to Callie. It was unusual for him to fall so quickly for a beautiful woman. She was a whole lot more than gorgeous, he knew, but he wouldn't have been so open to her in the city because his guard would have been up. He was successful in his practice. He had money and status. He attracted money-grubbers and social-climbers because of his title—Dr. Jake Lamb. Callie didn't even know he was doctor yet. She hadn't pried. She hadn't cared. She just treated him as another human being enjoying his time on a breathtaking island.

Jake didn't want to push Callie, but he had half a mind to cancel his own snorkeling charter and ask to join her, whatever she was doing. True, he had already learned a great deal about the island the day before; but what he really wanted to do was be with her, apologize for his prematurely forward behavior, and convince her that her reaction was okay. He hoped he would have time to do just that as they spent the evening together.

Admittedly, he wanted to do more of the same. What hot-blooded male wouldn't want to kiss and touch Callie again? Kissing her was like breathing in the fresh tropical air after a cleansing morning rain. Yet, the passion and heat behind the kiss was like the burn of the sun in the Caribbean afternoon.

He would be more patient this time, though, and let her lead the way. He definitely wanted more time with "Callie of the White Sand." That reminded him, he needed to learn her last name. All in due time, he thought as he continued his leisurely swim among the brain corals and graceful angelfish.

*I*t was two thirty. The waitress obliged him with another glass of iced tea, his third, and a friendly smile. He imagined she was wondering when he would actually order his lunch.

Callie was probably just running late. Surely she wasn't in any kind of trouble. Still, the thought that she had run into some grumpy salt-water crocodile or boa constrictor niggled at the back of his mind. He sat watching the door for another half-hour, becoming more worried by the minute. Callie struck him as a woman of her word. She wouldn't stand him up.

Something terrible might have happened to her. That was the thought that stuck with him as he paid the waitress for his four iced teas, left his photos forgotten at the drugstore, and raced off in his golf cart to Callie's bungalow.

He knocked at her door, praying that she was

home and safe and had simply forgotten about their rendezvous. The door was opened by a tiny Mestizo woman, dressed in a white "Visit Belize" t-shirt that reached her knees.

"Si, Señor? Can I help you?"

"Hi. I'm Jake. I'm here to see Callie. We had a date at the Pier and we missed each other."

"Oh. Well, I am sorry, Jake, but the young woman who was staying here left this morning. I am simply cleaning for the next guest." The woman left the doorway to return to her tasks.

Jake followed her past the threshold. She turned in alarm and then relaxed as she saw his stricken expression. The imposing man took in the empty bungalow. She watched the realization dawn on him as he acknowledged that the young woman had, indeed, left nothing behind. He looked as if he'd been jilted, the poor man.

"Did she leave any notes, do you know?" Jake became suddenly, inexplicably, angry at the situation, with Callie.

"I'm sorry, Señor. She left nothing."

"Thank you." With that, Jake took his leave. He'd be hard-pressed to explain how he felt just then. There was the fury, vile and unexpected, that she'd left him without explanation or warning. Yet they had only just met two days ago.. She had no obligation to him.

They did have a connection, though. He felt it as surely as he felt the fine sand slip between his toes and his flip-flops as he walked back to his golf cart. Now she was gone. Forever. He didn't even know her name. Raw disappointment consumed him.

*C*allie was ashamed and she was relieved. She knew that she was running away from her island sanctuary. She tried to convince herself it was because she really had stayed here too long. It was time to move on, to examine her options for living in the real world, to visit new possibilities.

She was running away from Jake Lamb. She decided during the sleepless night that her life would be far too complicated with Jake in it. Callie was always a loner. It would be easy to let Jake in, but then what? He would want to know everything. She would feel compelled to tell him. It would be like reliving her nightmare childhood all over again.

What if he was disgusted by her physical appearance, by her scars? Could she handle being rejected? By the time she revealed her innermost secrets, she knew she would love Jake. Part of her already did.

That was silly, though, wasn't it? One couldn't truly be in love after just two days. Callie didn't know where Jake was from, what he did for a living, or what sort of nasty habits hid behind his gentle façade. He was too good to be true. It was better to leave him behind.

Callie rose exhausted from her bed at five a.m., took a walk, in the opposite direction from Jake's bungalow this time, and watched the clock until 7 a.m. when she felt it would be a decent time to make a phone call. She called the only person in the States she could think of who would help her get settled, no questions asked; the only person who knew everything about Callie, start to finish. Except for the last six months—Callie hadn't been in touch with Leah since she'd left Seattle.

They had gone much longer than six months without talking before. It never mattered. Her friend was in San Francisco and Callie had thought of joining her there many times. It was an open invitation.

It took Callie about three hours to pack her things. She didn't have much, but she had accumulated enough that she had to be crafty to fit it all into her three bags.

She still had her filet of tuna, so she fried it up quickly for a late breakfast and then cleaned her kitchenette, tossing the other contents of her refrigerator into the trash.

She waited with her baggage for the next available water taxi to the mainland. She boarded the boat for Belize City at shortly after noon and by five o'clock, Pacific Time, she was at the San Jose International Airport.

Callie felt protected by her distance from the Caye. The change in landscape and pace served to remind her how far she had really removed herself from the life she'd grown up with. She was coming home, though to a very different city. New possibilities awaited her, and none so complicated as Jake Lamb.

As Callie took a taxi to the heart of San Francisco, she watched the passing buildings and cars with renewed fascination. Buildings imposed on the landscape as far as the eye could see, separated by bridges and choppy water. Green spaces were carefully manicured. Countless numbers of row houses sat dwarfed by glass and concrete, skyscraping giants.

Blue skies and fluffy cumulus clouds hovered over vivid contrasting colors of bridges and buildings. Much like her native Seattle, when it was sunny in the heart of San Francisco, people came outside in droves. Diversity sang out from the din. Humans of every race and shape and manner of dress roamed the busy sidewalks and dotted the hillsides of the city parks.

There were typical t-shirt clad, flip-flop adorned college students, as well as sharply-dressed, hurried business people, moms with babies in strollers, and panhandlers lining concrete walls and steps near buildings and businesses. Callie took it all in, silently wondering if she would feel at home here or if this was just another stop in the exploration of her listless life.

For a moment, with Jake, she felt as if she belonged with someone. Callie shrugged off the thought. That kind of intimacy was impossible, she knew, without giving in to the emotions she feared most.

As her taxi stopped in front of a whitewashed, stucco apartment building just a heartbeat from downtown, Callie spotted the one person who had managed to get past her carefully erected defense. A miserable childhood led her to Leah and Seattle Youth Alliance when she was fifteen. She told her lawyers everything when she sued her adoptive parents. Leah was an intern and a law student at the time.

Leah was the one she opened up to and entrusted with her painful secrets. Leah held her hand as they wheeled her into the operating room for her first skin graft as her burn treatment began ten years too late. Leah offered, over and over again, to be more than her mentor and her lawyer. She offered friendship, solace, and a place to stay, should Callie ever choose to accept these.

It took Callie more than seven years, but she finally decided to rely on Leah once again, and as her old friend enfolded her in her warm and waiting arms, Callie glimpsed, at last, the home she'd been looking for. It wasn't a place. It was an embrace. It was someone to rely on beside herself for once.

Chapter 5

*L*eah Kaye Foster Westfield arose at seven the next morning, exhausted from a late-night session with Callie (and a fruity bottle of wine,) but grateful that her reclusive friend had decided to rejoin civilization. Leah would have loved to sleep longer. She rolled over to give her Abyssinian cat, Beulah, an affectionate 'good-morning' pat, as she tried to clear away the cobwebs in her brain.

She had to be sharp today. Truth be told, she had to be sharp everyday. She had been given an exclusive chance at a Sports Medicine fellowship through *UCSF* and *St. Katherine's Hospital.* She worked and studied at a facility that treated complex sports-related injuries with state-of-the-art equipment and methods.

Her last patient the day before was a prima ballerina, touring with a world-famous troupe, who suffered chronic foot and ankle pain. Dealing with challenges such as these inspired Leah to continue her grueling, fourteen-hour days and her progress toward her career in Sports Medicine.

Leah groaned, as she glanced at her bloodshot eyes in the mirror of the hallway bathroom. She imagined her younger friend fared much better than she. Oh well, nothing a scalding shower and a few eyedrops couldn't fix, she thought.

Life hadn't been any less demanding six years ago when she'd first come to San Francisco as a brand-new lawyer, working for the District Attorney's office. Leah still worked unreasonably long, hectic days, trying to move her way through the ranks of a dozen ambitious law school graduates.

A climbing trip with one of these young lawyers changed the path of Leah's life forever. She and Scott Furlow were fast friends. They both moved from Washington State to San Francisco and the DA's office. He was from Spangle, Washington, just outside of Spokane. She was from Seattle.

They really had little in common. Scott was an avid outdoorsman, enjoying fishing, rock-climbing, and mountain biking. He was raised by conservative and devout Episcopalians. Leah grew up in a city apartment over a busy bookstore, buying her fish from the open-air market and considering the hike from downtown to Capitol Hill in Seattle the most strenuous outdoor exercise she would encounter. Her parents were lesbians.

Scott was charming, a small-town upbringing mingling with urban aspirations, in a young man who was as chivalrous and kind-hearted, as he was cutthroat and legally astute. She found out as she accompanied him to the gym after work, he also had a great set of abs.

He and Leah were both fiercely competitive and their willingness to pour effort into their work netted them both cases they could sink their teeth into. They often ended up being assigned to work together. A lukewarm romance ensued. Scott and Leah settled into a pattern of working together, dining together, and occasionally sleeping together, with neither having the energy or time to yearn for more from each other.

They took a vacation to Yosemite National Park on a holiday weekend, Labor Day. Scott wanted to get out of the city and to explore the trails of the beautiful park.

Leah tagged along, less for the thrill of being outdoors, and more for curiosity about a national treasure. Besides, Scott had bet her that, as a city-chick, she was incapable of making the taxing 2,700 feet climb to the top of Yosemite Fall. Leah hated to lose a bet.

Leah found the fresh air invigorating and the hike, although strenuous, breathtaking. They got to the top of the trail after dusk and Scott insisted on going off-trail to camp until they could descend in the morning. It began to get windy shortly after, as the sky grew darker. They would have settled in for a peaceful evening in their pup tent if it weren't for the phenomenon of the Mono winds. Scott simply stepped away from the campsite for a few minutes before bed to relieve himself and a seventy mile per hour wind gust blew him off a twenty-foot rock face onto a shelf below.

Leah heard only his terrified scream and a muffled cry of pain a few moments later, coming from much further away. She noticed the windy gales getting stronger and stayed low to the ground as she searched for Scott. With her meager flashlight, Leah could detect the drop-off from which the early fall leaves were swept away with Scott among them.

She lay on her stomach and pulled herself to the edge of the cliff, as close as she dared go in the darkness. She yelled to Scott, who only moaned a reply. He was obviously unable to move, and she was completely unable to help him as the cloak of the night closed in around her.

Leah returned to the tent site only to find that her cell phone had no reception in that area. Being a holiday weekend, Leah's best hope was to find another hiker who could go for help. She had no familiarity with the terrain and the winds had her terrified that she would find the same fate as Scott.

Leah hiked the quarter mile back to the main trail,

crouching much of the way and bracing herself against the stiff wind. Unbeknownst to either hiker, the high winds were predicted by park officials just two hours earlier and they shut off trails in the Yosemite Valley area due to the unseasonably early onset of the Mono winds. Leah and Scott were the last climbers to reach the summit that day and the trailheads would not reopen for another two days.

Leah huddled against a boulder, praying for a passerby, trying to shelter as best as she could against the westward gales. She even called upon the spirit of Sister Ellen, a Catholic nun who had been like a grandmother to her during her Seattle upbringing, to bring help for Scott.

Dawn's light hadn't come soon enough for Leah. The minute she was able to see, she crept back to the tent site and peered over the edge of the drop-off. The morning was silent as a tomb and she saw Scott laying in his lime green climbing gear just to the right of a scraggly evergreen some twenty feet below. His bed was a pile of jagged rocks and his legs lay twisted at odd angles to his torso. It wasn't quite light enough to see his eyes, but Leah guessed that Scott was most likely unconscious. Or dead.

Leah shook off the thought. She clung to the hope that there was still time to get help. Daylight revealed an overland route to Scott's location. Leaving their gear behind and taking only water, her cell phone, and the first-aid kit, she returned to the trail for five hundred yards and then veered off the path to the left, ignoring scratches from the heavy brush as she worked her way back to Scott.

She arrived at his location in time to hear him moan softly. He was alive, but hurt very badly. Leah guessed the only thing that saved Scott's life during his treacherous fall was the fact that he hadn't yet removed his climbing gear. His helmet rested atop his head still, though it had completely split down the middle. He'd landed on his back, so she guessed that he must certainly have done damage in that area. She knew better than to try and move him.

Besides, he was about six inches taller than she and outweighed her by at least fifty pounds. His legs were obviously useless to him. The left leg even had a bone protruding against the flesh, a sight that made the bile rise from her empty stomach to her dry throat.

Leah attempted to rouse Scott and put the water to his mouth to prevent dehydration, and she received a painful moan in exchange for her efforts. For the first time in her young life, Leah was totally unable to come up with a solution to their very treacherous situation. She'd always prided herself on her calm and quick thinking in crisis situations.

But Leah was completely ignorant about first aid and even less knowledgeable about the outdoors. For all she knew, she could leave to find help, only to have a mountain lion feast upon her disabled friend. She realized, though, that leaving him was a risk she would have to take, because she had no idea how to treat his grave injuries. She had to go for help.

She left her sock stuffed into a bush where she emerged onto the main trail, so that she could find Scott's location once more. It was almost eight miles to the trailhead, and Leah hiked her fastest down the steep trail in still dangerously high winds, when she finally met a park official about three-quarters of the way down. The ranger was surprised to see a hiker, and was even more surprised to find her without any gear.

Leah gave him details about Scott and he radioed for help. By the time the ranger and Leah reached Scott's location, the rescue team was also well on their way. The winds were too high for a helicopter rescue, so the team came via land. All had a wealth of experience scaling the Yosemite Valley trails, so they arrived soon after Leah and the ranger.

Once the emergency medical technicians arrived, Leah realized how inadequate her first aid treatment was for Scott. Using her first aid kit, the workers first draped Scott with a thermal cover, explaining that he was probably hypothermic and in shock after spending the night in the open with such injuries. The blanket helped alleviate those immediate dangers.

They braced Scott's neck and placed him gingerly on a backboard, as he stayed eerily silent. An intravenous line was placed and a bag attached to replace Scott's lost fluids. They could only hope that he had no internal bleeding working against them. Again with materials from her own first aid kit, the workers bandaged obvious scrapes and splinted Scott's left leg.

Leah watched the whole process with interest and dismay. She hated feeling helpless and stupid when it came to basic first aid techniques. Luckily, despite it all, Scott was still alive.

He would survive, despite three broken vertebrae, pelvic fractures, three broken bones in his legs, a collapsed lung, and a serious concussion. He bruised his kidneys, but thankfully, there was no internal bleeding. Painful rehabilitation brought Scott very near to his former physical health. He and Leah remained friends, but no more, after his recovery.

Leah vowed to herself, at his side in that hospital room, that she would never, ever be that inept again. She'd enjoyed learning the law, but her knowledge in this field could do nothing to take care of the immediate needs of someone who was hurt or ill. It suddenly seemed so much nobler to fix this sort of problem, instead of spending time trying to nail slippery criminals to the wall in a system filled with loopholes.

Latent trauma and close self-examination had Leah applying for immediate admission to medical school. She gained acceptance for the spring quarter to the University of California San Francisco and, before long, Leah's life veered onto a totally different path toward a most admirable profession: The practice of medicine.

*F*ive years later, Leah examined herself in the mirror. She was now, proudly, Dr. Leah Westfield and she was bedecked in sweatpants and a t-shirt on her way to *St. Katherine's* where she would don scrubs and a labcoat for her day in the Sports Medicine department. She pulled her shoulder-length red hair into a wet twist and secured it with a clip. She put concealer on the dark circles under her eyes, frowning about the frequent appearances these were making since she'd turned thirty a few years before. She put gloss on her lips, foregoing any other makeup for time's sake.

She toasted a bagel to eat on the BART and she filled her thermos with stiff black coffee from her automatic drip. She wrote a note of 'Good Morning' to her houseguest, telling Callie where to find other breakfast ingredients.

Leah felt the familiar pull of her new job and grinned again at her good fortune, knowing that the choices she'd made along the way were completely right for her. She was dog-tired this morning, but she was still pumped about what the coming day at the hospital would bring.

She slipped on a robin's-egg blue zip-up sweatshirt, slung her canvas bag over her shoulder, and exited her apartment building to a blanket of early morning fog. The skip in her step carried her the two blocks to her transit stop. She was right on time for her seven forty-five ride. It was going to be a great day.

Chapter 6

Callie awoke from her slumber at ten o'clock in a panic. The broad windows of the second-floor apartment were encased in smoke. She bolted out of bed, heart racing, searching desperately for the nearest escape, not knowing which way to go.

She realized momentarily, though, that she neither smelled nor tasted the acrid air that smoke produced. She was all too familiar with both, even seventeen years later. Instead, she smelled sweet pea and fresh brewed coffee. She sought to calm herself, ignored the flight response that gripped her, and moved closer to the south-facing window. As she peered toward the street below, she realized with a shaky sigh that what she saw outside was fog.

Leah's apartment was in the Inner Sunset neighborhood, which, according to Leah, was friendly and funky and eclectic, with affordable rental rates. It was also famous for being the foggiest neighborhood in San Francisco proper. This was a typical Inner Sunset morning. Callie finally relaxed and smoothed down her hair and nightgown.

She glanced at the clock and groaned as she realized that the combination of the time change and weariness from her late night had made her sleep far later than she intended. She knew that Leah would be leaving early for the hospital and she wanted to send her off. Resigned to her mistake, she padded into the kitchen to find the coffee pot still warm and accompanied by Leah's cheerful note.

Callie poured herself a cup and greeted Beulah, who made herself comfortable on Leah's glass-topped dining table. She took a sip and grimaced. The brew was practically thick enough to chew! She supposed Leah's long nights in medical school and residency necessitated strong coffee. Callie grabbed the fat-free soymilk from the fridge and diluted her coffee to taste.

She was used to drinking tropical juice or eating native fruit first thing in the morning in Belize, but the hot drink seemed more suited to her new surroundings. She noticed that Leah had left the morning paper on the table. It sat on a placemat, inviting her to read. She had to chuckle, though, because the unopened issue looked exactly like twenty others that were stacked in various places around the kitchen area. She doubted if Leah ever found time to actually read the paper she subscribed to.

Callie sat and read the paper, familiarizing herself with local and national news. One thing was sure about being back in the States: Frenzy was created by the media over truly insignificant happenings. They made a complete circus out of her lawsuit against her adoptive parents. She wasn't sure why a child's suffering made compelling news, but she resented the intrusion then and she barely skimmed those kinds of stories now.

Similarly, she didn't really find it all that gripping to know how much water and electricity were being consumed by the governor's mansion. Apparently liberal Californians had found a new area for scrutiny of public officials.

In a way, it was refreshing to escape to her island paradise, just to know what it was like to forget about the grind and stress of the American way of life. She could have continued and maybe she should have, except there had been Jake.

Jake. She had actually tried to put him out of her mind since her arrival. She hadn't told Leah her reason for leaving, only glossing over a desire to return to life as normal.

She put the paper aside as an unexpected wave of longing broad-sided her. Callie tried not to acknowledge it, but she felt it, nonetheless. Jake was so charming, so easy to talk to, so strikingly handsome. She wanted him with a fierceness that abandoned reason.

He was probably furious with her. She realized with a quick stab of regret that she'd never given him any information about herself, not even her last name. Any hope that he might track her down was dashed by her hasty exit.

She reminded herself that it was for the best. Living here with Leah for a while would help her further put her life in order. She needed a career, a purpose, before jumping into a relationship. Maybe she could defeat her demons. Perhaps by the time she met the next exceptional male, she would be ready to accept all of the risks that would come with loving him. She just hoped that she would be lucky enough to meet someone like Jake again.

Callie picked up the paper once more and carried it to the worn creamy leather sofa and sat with her legs under her, gathering her robe around her as she pored over "Help Wanted" ads.

*T*he chilly September fog finally lifted at one o'clock. Callie circled a number of ads that showed promise, from personal assistant to medical receptionist. She would borrow Leah's computer in the morning and start to put her resume out to some of them. She finally showered and dressed at noon.

Her wardrobe of gauzy, cottony clothes didn't fit her

needs for the impending fall in San Francisco. She had a pair of medium-weight khakis and a ruby-colored knit top buried deep in her suitcase and she donned these for an early afternoon exploration of Leah's neighborhood. She decided to shop a little, for some warmer clothes and a few professional-appearing outfits for future interviews.

She wanted to make Leah dinner. She knew from her conversation with Leah the night before that Leah rarely made it home until almost nine o'clock. It had to be a torturously long day for her friend, but she knew Leah thrived on it. Callie also knew that Leah rarely ate properly as a result of her long hours. Leah had always been petite, but now she was downright skinny.

Callie was going to fix Leah the biggest load of calories she could summon. She had learned a wonderful coconut-lime chicken recipe from the old Garafunan clerk on Caye Caulker. Along with that, she would fix garlic-laced mashed potatoes and creamed artichoke hearts. She would also make an almond mocha layer cake for dessert. A bottle of Napa Valley Chardonnay would nicely accompany it all.

Callie had plenty of time to kill in between, so she shopped leisurely, enjoying the friendly shop owners and the upbeat neighborhood. People here seemed to really know one another, something that struck her as unusual in such a large city. She also learned that the celebratory atmosphere of the retail section came from the fact that the fog had lifted for the day, bringing patrons and tourists to their part of the city.

She noticed "Help Wanted" signs, some in the windows of boutiques and a hardware store. The nearby corner grocery also advertised for help. Callie considered these, and rejected the idea, knowing that working in retail meant odd hours and honed customer service abilities. After observing the outgoing clerks and bustling traffic of these places, Callie knew she was far too reserved to work here, despite the convenience to Leah's apartment.

Callie returned to the apartment at five and started her preparations for dinner. She baked the cake first so it could cool before she frosted it. As she prepared the shrimp for their lime juice and coconut milk bath, flicking flakes of crimson chili pepper from the cutting board into the mixing bowl, Callie's thoughts turned once again to the island and to Jake.

She flushed as she remembered Jake's searing lips on hers, the way he stepped into her, fitting her feminine softness perfectly into the hard muscles of his body. Then Callie quickly shook away the thoughts and swore off red pepper flakes. The heat of the peppers must have been the reason for her lustful recollection.

Callie enjoyed her ministrations with the rest of dinner. She peeled potatoes and steamed artichokes, tying up her capable hands. The kitchen filled with enticing smells of the tropics—coffee, coconut, citrus. She put on the satellite radio and found a blend of hits from her childhood in the nineties and she sang along, musing once in a while at Beulah, who had planted herself on the back of the sofa to watch Callie's every move. Her ears would go back when Callie hit a particularly high note, but she never left her post, enthralled as she was with her guest dancing and bobbing around her owner's kitchen.

Callie put each dish in the oven warmer as she finished it, preparing herself for Leah's late arrival. As it turned out, Leah was a little earlier than usual. She flew into the apartment in a cascade of auburn hair, her canvas rucksack stuffed to the gills with research material on rotator cuff injuries of the shoulder. She was bent on getting a quick dinner and brief visit with Callie, but what she really needed to figure out was what to do with a San Francisco *49er*'s football player who needed at least ten degrees more range of motion in his shoulder before his trainer would allow him to play.

Leah paused in the entry as she realized that her apartment smelled absolutely delicious. Leah's mouth immediately began to water.

Callie, bless her, was flushed with her dinner-making efforts, looking every inch like an exotic Snow White after she'd cleaned the dwarfs' abode. "Welcome home! I'm glad you're early. Are you hungry?" Callie greeted her new roommate cheerfully.

"I'm starving, Callie. What did you do? Did you cook all day, just for us? It smells divine in here."

"It didn't take all day. I actually did some shopping and checked out the neighborhood. I need to use your computer in the morning, if you'll let me, because I think I found some interesting jobs in the paper too."

"You've been really busy for your first day!"

"Not any busier than you, I bet," Callie replied.

Callie sat on the leather sofa with one foot under her body, and then popped up again as she asked, "Can I get you a glass of Chardonnay?"

"I would love a glass, but then I'll have to stop. Did you leave the coffee in the pot from this morning? I think I'm going to need it to wade through the research I brought home."

Callie handed Leah a cool glass of buttery Chardonnay. "It's a good thing tomorrow's Friday, Leah. Between our late night and your plans for this evening, you're going to need the weekend to catch up on your sleep."

"Aw, Callie, sleep's overrated, didn't you know that? That's one of the first things they teach us in medical school—first, how important sleep is to the body's overall health and well-being, and second, how we need to get over our basic need for it, because we're not going to get much sleep for five or six years."

"Well if you need to study tonight, then we'd better get started on dinner."

"I guess so. I want to spend more time with you, Callie. Maybe Sunday we can make plans."

"I'd like that, but only if you have time. I'll be here for a while. I'm not going anywhere, except for maybe to a real job."

"You don't really need to work do you, what with the Justice's money in your pocket?" Leah knew better than anyone what kind of money Callie had gotten from her lawsuit.

"That's blood money, Leah. I want to earn my own way for once. The Justices locked me away from the world for nearly ten years before I realized that my confinement wasn't normal. They took me in as a gravely injured little girl and doped me up and claimed to the world and insurance companies that they were making me all better."

"But they weren't, were they, Callie?" Leah knew more than anyone how Callie had suffered.

"Nope. They pocketed the money and they went out and partied with their socialite friends. I never really had parents, Leah. No amount of money is going to make up for that."

"I have never figured out why they adopted you, Callie. Were they compassionate at first and then they saw dollar signs?"

"I think I've been trying to find that answer myself for way too long. I have to let all of that go, Leah. If I don't, I might never build a life on my own. I just keep searching for answers, in vain."

"How can I help?"

"I'm just grateful that you're letting me stay until I figure it out. I met a guy, you know, while I was in Belize," Callie confessed.

"Oh really? Is that why you left?" Leah was intuitive enough to know that Callie was running from something when she arrived. She was like a cat with a coyote at her tail when she exited the taxi. It was only this evening that she finally seemed to relax.

"I think so. Yes. I told myself that it was time to leave the island, but the truth is I probably would have stayed longer if my mystery man hadn't scared me away."

"Why did he frighten you? I would give anything to have a 'mystery man' show up!" Leah laughed ruefully.

"I only knew him two days, Leah, but he had the most incredible smile and he was a gentleman and he kissed me."

"What a crime. And only on the second date even," Leah teased.

"I've never wanted anyone like that, Leah." Callie remained serious.

"I don't get it. What's wrong with wanting someone?"

With this, Callie slid her top to one side to uncover her right shoulder. She revealed a hideous scar, the skin stretched and webbed across her shoulder, chest, and arm. Leah was transfixed. She had thought Callie had all of her burns surgically repaired. Her face and neck were fantastic. She couldn't even tell that, at fifteen, the right side of Callie's face had still been significantly disfigured. But her body was obviously another story. A tear slid unchecked down Callie's cheek. Her misery spoke volumes and she didn't have to say a word.

Leah took Callie in her arms and stroked her hair as she said, "That can be fixed too, Callie. Just give it time."

"I'm tired of surgeries, Leah. I've had more than thirty. I feel like one giant skin graft. These can be hidden."

"Unless you're intimate with someone."

"Exactly."

"Well I would have run away too," Leah admitted. "But someday you're going to have to work on this. You know, I'm good friends with a burn specialist. I recommend him highly. He's on vacation, but maybe you can see him when he gets back. You can't go through life all alone, Callie."

"That's why I have you. We'll see about the rest later." Callie smiled winningly and Leah gave her another hug. "Let's have dinner."

As Callie pulled out and dished up one delicious dish after another, Leah realized how nice it would be to have her friend around for a while. Not only was she a wonderful cook, she seemed to understand Leah's time crunch. She would make a good roommate.

In exchange, Leah would do her best to help Callie to move past the burns and the barriers and the horrible, painful battleground that had been her childhood. It was time for Callie to heal.

Chapter 7

*T*he prisoner watched with detached amusement as the fight at hand escalated from angry words to fists and homemade knives, sharpened from the handles of spoons, magically appeared in the two mens' hands. These men would definitely wind up in the infirmary if neither of them ended up dead.

He shuddered involuntarily. Life was so easily taken, intentionally or not. He imagined the two angry black youths fighting right now had little regard for life's fragility. They'd likely lived most of their lives on the streets, raised in fatherless homes, taught by adversity to respect and trust no one. His childhood had been a little bit like that, but he was old and wise enough to know that this was no excuse.

There was no nobility, no satisfaction in taking a life. Quite the opposite—responsibility churned up his gut to the point of sending him to the infirmary at times. The dead were the lucky ones, though.

He fought the urge to throw his spent, glowing cigarette into the garbage barrel where it would light the contents causing a small fire and a stir in the exercise yard. Fire still gripped him, caused him yearning like no wanton woman had ever done. He was on his best behavior, though, his hopes high that it would buy him freedom before he got too old to enjoy it. He stamped out the glowing ember on the butt and placed it in the sand of the 'butt barrel.'

Yep, survivors had it much harder than victims. Guilt ate at you like an intestinal parasite. He knew one of his most glorious fires had left just one survivor. He'd made a mistake. He'd only made a few and the other had landed him here.

He wondered for the thousandth time about that survivor. Did she feel as lucky as she was to have been rescued? Did she know about him and did she hate him as much as he hated himself for what he'd done to her family? Mostly he wondered if his culpability and remorse could ever compensate for leaving her all alone in the world.

Chapter 8

*D*r. Sean O'Carroll felt distracted. What he really needed to do was finish his morning rounds with his post-operative sports medicine patients and be on his way to the rehab wing for his first morning outpatient appointment, which started at nine-thirty.

Nine o'clock and he tried his best to pay attention to the hockey player who'd had an arthroscopic repair of his knee the afternoon before. The man really needed to be up and walking by now, but his pain was apparently preventing him from doing so. Really, hockey players, for being so tough on the ice, could be so intolerant when it came to an injury such as this. He wrote an order absently for an increase of pain medication and then asked the nurse to get crutches and make the man's first post-surgical walk a priority.

He'd no sooner finished making these orders and his mind wandered once again to the gorgeous redhead he had encountered the day before in the rehab unit. They had literally bumped into each other, both with their heads down, each concentrating on a patient chart instead of where each was going. Sean was six feet tall, as opposed to the redhead's five foot three. Their first encounter had been a flurry of flying charts and flailing limbs as he tried to catch the young woman before she took a serious fall.

He was embarrassed at his clumsiness. Then, as the smell of her lavender shampoo reached his nose and he saw her beguiling eyes and fiery hair, Sean had been horrified once again to find himself caught off guard. She was like a wood nymph—tiny, fresh, and lovely—and she had come out of nowhere. He'd never seen her before at *St. Katherine's* and he was acquainted with just about everyone there.

Dr. Sean O'Carroll was an orthopedic surgeon. It was well known among San Franciscans that he was the best, particularly for active, sports-minded individuals who wanted to maintain an elite level of activity beyond surgery. He'd worked tirelessly for his fifteen-year career at *St. Katherine's*, building a solid reputation and gaining the utmost respect from his medical peers.

He admitted being a tyrant in the operating room, coolly demanding only the best nurses and surgical techs to help him achieve what he considered the highest art form he could produce—a healthy post-surgical joint or spine.

Most of his coworkers feared and revered him. They hardly knew him at all. If he had a life outside of the hospital, he was intensely private about it. Most of them had noticed a simple gold band on his finger for much of his career, so they had assumed he was married, but he'd never appeared at hospital social functions, so nobody had ever actually seen his spouse.

Then, mysteriously, a few years ago, the band had disappeared. Either he'd decided that it was too much of a hassle to wear it and remove it for surgery, or he had gone through a divorce. Since his methods and manner never changed at his workplace, his coworkers could only guess.

In fact, Sean was single, though he would never have shared that fact with any of his staff or other physicians. He believed a private life was just that—private. He'd been blessed with the ability to shrug his home-life off with his outdoor jacket and put his professional cloak on with his lab coat.

When he'd still been finishing his orthopedics rotation, Sean was annoyed by other resident doctors obsessing over their personal lives and he vowed never to muddle his work with such musings on his own part.

That was why he was so completely stymied by his gut reaction to the young lady he'd run into the day before. She was a fellow in Sports Medicine; he could tell by her nametag. It also said her name was Dr. Westfield. She was a student and she was off-limits and he'd never, ever (before now) given a second thought to dating a coworker.

So why was he still thinking about her nearly twenty-four hours later? Perhaps it was the sucker-punch that was her easy smile as he reddened and mumbled an apology. She looked at him frankly, intelligently, not with the usual edge of fear with which most students regarded him. Then she held out her left hand for her chart, which he'd picked up for her, and her right hand in introduction.

She had a firm, cool grip and she simply said, "You must be the famous Dr. O'Carroll. I'm pleased to finally meet you. I'm Leah."

Leah was like so many other medical graduates these days, using her first name with her colleagues instead of addressing herself as "Doctor." Sean had never acquired the same habit. He mumbled something incoherent and impersonal instead of introducing himself, and continued on his way.

Leah simply shrugged and continued her business as well. She hadn't noticed him round the corner and then peer back around it and study her profile as she paused at the appointment desk. Even her features were petite, her cheeks and nose fine-boned. She was a slip of a thing in her big scrubs, perhaps too thin, but with curves showing through in the right places.

Sean had realized he was staring and had quickly gathered his lanky body back around the corner before she sensed him watching her.

*H*e would watch her, though. Leah had already made fast friends with many of her coworkers at *St. Katherine's* and they were the first to notice that the enigmatic Dr. Sean O'Carroll paying undue attention to the pretty young fellowship student.

He was so serious and stern that many of them thought he was too old for spunky Leah; but then none of them would have placed her age at thirty-two. They issued warnings to her about Dr. O'Carroll, told stories, and aired rumors that had flown around about him for years.

Leah found herself watching him too. He was slender and tall, with pleasantly broad shoulders resulting from his very physical job. Up close, his eyes were a riot of green and amber, but she knew that lovely hazel turned hard when he wore his professional visage. His thick shock of white hair also made him appear much more mature than his forty-four years, but his face was smooth and boyish and Leah thought he must be much younger than he appeared at first glance.

She had also observed him with a rehab patient whom he'd treated repeatedly for lower back injuries. He was gentle and kind with her. She was a retired professional tennis player and Leah knew from conversation that the patient worshipped Dr. O'Carroll.

Leah could only hope to be as reputable and accomplished as Dr. O'Carroll someday. She'd always borne her emotions very close to the surface. Her moms told her it was a side-effect of having red hair. Years of law school and medical school had finally taught her temperance. She was just professional enough to be gaining the respect of her peers, but just sweet enough to be endearing to them as well.

She didn't believe that Dr. O'Carroll could be as cool or as intimidating as he pretended to be, nor did she heed her colleagues' warnings about him. She'd gotten under his skin. She met his glances and assessments with bold challenge and clear, unspoken invitations. Dr. Leah Westfield was going to be his undoing.

Sean O'Carroll was terrified of what that might mean.

Leah was working a rare Sunday in October, trying to get caught up on her outpatient charting, when she felt eyes boring into the back of her head. She turned quickly to find Dr. O'Carroll looking her directly in the eyes. He cleared his throat and began to flip through the chart in his hand. There was nobody else around at the central rehab kiosk, so Leah decided to take a chance.

"It's quiet this morning, isn't it?" Leah asked softly, not wanting to startle Dr. O'Carroll.

He gave her a look very much like the proverbial 'deer in the headlights.' He cleared his throat once again and looked discreetly around him before he answered. "Yes, it is rather peaceful," Sean replied, his deep timbre matching Leah's low tone.

"One of the occupational therapists told me it would be. That's why I came in to catch up. It's much easier when you don't have to wade through three other doctors or nurses to find a chart."

"I have to agree with you there." Sean returned to looking at his chart, feigning interest, but actually absorbing nothing of its contents.

Leah refused to be dismissed so easily this time. She moved her chart to the desk directly beneath the raised countertop at which he was standing. She looked up at him and watched him shift uncomfortably.

"Dr. O'Carroll?"

"Yes, um, Dr. Westfield?"

"You can call me 'Leah.'"

"Very well then. Yes, Leah?"

She smiled then, mischievously, and Sean's breathing hitched uncomfortably. "You don't like me much, do you, Dr. O'Carroll?"

"Well, that would be difficult to say. I haven't worked with you directly, since you specialize in rehabilitation and I'm a surgeon."

"Then why do I make you so uncomfortable? I've noticed the sour looks you've been giving me when I see you staring." No one was around to chase him off, so she was going to get to the bottom of this.

"I have not been staring, Dr. Westfield, er, Leah," he replied.

"You have. May I call you 'Sean'?"

Sean studied Leah's expression and realized that she was enjoying this banter. She wasn't at all angry with him. She was amused. 'Now what?' He thought helplessly.

"I don't usually let students call me by my first name, Leah."

"Yes, but you don't usually pay much attention to these students either, do you?"

"What makes you think that I'm paying any special attention to you? Is this your ego that we're talking about?"

Leah was nonplussed. He had been watching her. Her colleagues had noticed it. Then she had second thoughts. What if she was wrong about the glances he'd been giving her. She reddened slightly. "I didn't mean to be presumptuous, Doctor. Some of my coworkers had suggested that you were paying more attention to me than to other students, and I guess I shouldn't have listened to them."

"No, Dr. Westfield, you should not have listened.

Rumors can be vicious here at *St. Katherine's* and I can honestly say that I've been the subject of many because I refuse to be candid about my life outside these walls. You may want to take heed of my policy."

"With all due respect," Leah replied now, coldly, "I wouldn't want to be like you, Dr. O'Carroll. While your work is admirable and your patients love you, your coworkers think you nothing short of a snob. I would rather be deemed professionally competent and also be loved and trusted by the people I work with.

"You've obviously never been taught how to attract help instead of commanding it. I won't have to work nearly so hard as you because my coworkers will want to help me. I am who I am, *Sean* O'Carroll and I don't plan to take any advice from you."

Sean was wounded, but he knew that every word she said was true. He wasn't going to let her see this weakness, though. Perhaps this was his chance to be rid of her influence on him. "I must insist that you remain professional with your seniors here, Dr. Westfield. You will address me as 'Doctor' and I will do the same. I trust that we won't have another conversation like this."

"That's guaranteed; but I don't want to keep looking up to find your Irish eyes scrutinizing me, Doctor. From now on, I expect you will leave me alone."

Sean nodded in agreement, but could say nothing. It would be easier if Dr. Leah Westfield hated him, the way others did. It was unfortunate that he felt as if he'd been pierced through the heart. He walked away, suddenly bereft. He hadn't felt this wretched since Gretchen had left him.

Leah watched Sean O'Carroll as he walked coolly away from her. He was certainly more conceited than she'd given him credit for. Why, then, did she think she had seen his proud shoulders slump as he approached the corner?

Leah finished her last chart hastily, anticipating her meeting with Callie at *B's Diner*. Her friend and new roommate was much more fun to be around than stuffy old Dr. O'Carroll anyway. They were going to eat lunch and go shopping at the factory outlets. Callie needed clothes for her new job and Leah was happy to act as fashion consultant.

She tried hard to anticipate the adventures ahead and to forget the piercing hazel eyes and the woodsy scent of her new nemesis.

Chapter 9

*C*allie didn't have to look very far or very long for a job. It turned out that Leah's moms, who owned a popular new and used bookstore on Capitol Hill in Seattle, also had old connections in San Francisco. There was a bookstore twelve blocks from Leah's apartment that needed a restocking clerk for just five hours a day on weekdays.

It was the kind of work Callie was looking for: Not too social, not too many hours, but yet requiring some intelligence and thought. She categorized new shipments into genres throughout the large store, which had been settled into a stately two-story Victorian. She made her way among the crowded stacks and reading nooks to nestle each new title into its temporary home.

Callie was also responsible for assembling displays and attracting the attention of potential buyers to a particular new title. She enjoyed the challenges and creativity that her job required. She liked that it allowed her to work independently.

She worked Monday through Friday from six until eleven in the morning, when the store opened to the public. Her boss was an eccentric, effeminate, and extremely well read, middle-aged man by the name of V.J. Banks. He tended to his minions lightly, visiting the store often, usually in the early morning hours and sometimes in the evenings.

V.J. had four successful bookstores in the city, all

named according to his initials, Callie's branch being *Victorian Juxtapositions*.

His sexual preferences aside, he also admired the feminine form, simply for the soft and simply mysterious presence it brought to the world. V.J. was intrigued by Callie the minute he met her. His old and dear friend from Seattle, Shirley Foster, had called him to recommend the young woman, who was a friend of her daughter's. Leah was a friend and patron from way back and he was happy to help her roommate.

There was something so sad and withdrawn about Callie that piqued V.J.'s curiosity. She did a fantastic job creatively with his displays and in rearranging the stacks to accommodate the plethora of new titles that arrived each week. V.J. frequented *Victorian Juxtapositions* to watch Callie work.

Callie would often be so absorbed in her work that she didn't pay attention to V.J.'s slender, fair-haired presence as he would sit at a café chair or reading settee watching her and drinking his morning latte. He made frequent, quiet compliments on the improvements she was making, but he never intruded on her concentration.

Callie grew used to V.J.'s pale-eyed scrutiny, and to his delight, began to actually communicate with him while she worked, asking him questions about the bookselling business and about his interest in reading. He found her refreshingly intelligent and crafty, as she picked his brain as a reader and consumer of books, helping her find new ways to attract customers to the titles she displayed.

V.J. never probed into Callie's life. He could tell that she was intensely private, haunted almost and he didn't wish to scare her off. He and Callie were becoming friends.

She was placing books on a low shelf, sitting Indian-style when V.J. took mercy on her young joints and handed her the last of the titles to put on the shelf. She looked over her shoulder at him and smiled.

"You look rather like a yoga-master making like a pretzel," he joked, feigning a grimace as he straightened.

"It is good exercise. *Victorian Juxtapositions* has some seriously low-slung shelving. You know, you could sell more of these books if you put more shelving at eye level," Callie suggested.

"Splendid idea, but where do you propose to put this shelving? This store is already jammed."

"You're right. It is entirely too well stocked and I have ideas for fixing that too, but that's a separate problem. You have some gorgeous nineteenth century paintings, and while they add to the homey atmosphere, I think you could put some classy walnut shelves under them and use bookends to display hardback titles.

"There are also some wider aisles between standing shelves. You don't want to put in more standing shelves and make the aisles too narrow, but you could put up some shelves that suspend from the ceiling and make them with steel cables and plexi-glass so that the storage is still there, but the visual space is still just as wide.

"I also have some ideas for lighting. Have you ever used track lighting with the new halogen bulbs?" She was enthusiastic, talking more than V.J. had ever heard her talk. He delighted in her enthusiasm.

"Draw up some plans, Callie and tell me the materials you have in mind and it's as good as done. Where did you learn so much about design?"

"I had a lot of time to myself when I was a kid. I spent hours pondering how I would reorganize my room and my house if I had the opportunity. I even sketched my ideas sometimes. My parents wouldn't let me go out to shop for materials, though."

"Why ever not?"

"It's a long story, V.J.," Callie replied, suddenly less

enthused.

"Well, Callie, it just happens to be lunch time and you've officially been given the 'Two-Hour V.J. Break.' I've got to hear this story."

They walked two doors down to a vegan café and took their seat in a private booth. V.J. ordered veggie and hummus pitas and Perrier's for both of them. He sat patiently and looked at Callie and said, "Okay. Do tell."

"I might as well start at the beginning."

"That usually works best," he agreed as he leaned his chin on one graceful hand.

"My life stopped and started when I was five. One day I was playing soccer in the yard with my brothers and eating Mom's homemade cookies, and then that night there was a terrifying fire, and the next day they were all gone."

"*All* of them, Callie?" V.J. was aghast.

"Yes. My mother and father, my two brothers and my little sister. I was the only survivor."

Intuitively, V.J. knew this weighed heavily on Callie. "Why do you suppose you were meant to survive?"

"So I could think of new and wonderful décor for the *V.J's* stores?" Callie offered weakly.

"Seriously, dear. I want to know this about you, Callie. My heart breaks for what you went through as a little girl."

"I know one thing I was not meant to be," Callie replied.

"And what is that?"

"I was not meant to be anyone's daughter. I said that my life stopped and started when I was five. I lost my real family only to be adopted by Cyrus and Constance Justice. Here I was, severely burned and orphaned, and they took pity on me and took me in."

"Were they loving parents?"

"At first they were. Constance had me make shopping lists. She bought me every kind of junk food I wanted. She outfitted me like a princess. They had no other children. I got to pick out the colors and furniture for my room—I chose purple. Cyrus was attentive, concerned that I be kept pain-free. What they knew and I didn't was that I could be kept comfortable and heal without ever having my burns fixed."

"How bad were these burns?"

"The entire right side of my body was affected, but the worst burns were to my chest, neck, right arm and face. I could show you, V.J., but, believe me, it's best left to the imagination.

"I couldn't very well be taken out in public with my appearance such as it was, so Constance and Cyrus chose to isolate me, confine me to the house. Then their real work started. I'm not sure whose brainchild this was, but they decided that money could be made off of my misery. They falsified medical and surgical documents to make it look to the insurance company like I'd had burn treatments done, and they pocketed the money."

V.J. couldn't contain his disdain. "Stinking vultures. This world has far too many of them. How old were you when you finally figured it out?"

"I was thirteen when I started gathering papers, copying them, building evidence. I got lawyers—that's how I met Leah, and I successfully sued them for just about everything they had, a rich doctor and his therapist wife."

"You must be loaded, Callie dear. Why am I paying for lunch again?"

She gave him a playful swat on his forearm. He really was a dear man. She took a deep breath. She couldn't remember the last time she had unloaded like this. Somehow she knew, though, that V.J. would understand her baggage.

"There's still one thing I don't understand," V.J. admitted.

"What's that?" Callie took a drink of her Perrier, fingering the loose edge of the label. She looked up to see V.J. studying her closely.

"You have the most lovely face. I'd have had no idea that you were subject to such childhood trauma. Did you have surgery, then, after all?"

"Many, many surgeries, V.J. and thank you. I've only recently begun to accept that I look normal to most people."

"Oh, Callie, you are leaps beyond normal. You're gorgeous. I have only just learned, though, that you are also extraordinarily courageous and bright."

Callie felt tears tugging at the corners of her eyes. "That means a lot, V.J.."

"Anytime, Callie." V.J. winked and raised his glass in silent tribute. "Can we move onto lighter fare now, though? I'm afraid I must know where you bought those espadrilles you're wearing."

Callie laughed as the tears dissipated and she bantered over fashion and alfalfa sprouts with her newest friend.

*B*y the time Callie had been at *V.J.'s* for two months, she considered the man himself almost as much her confidante as Leah. It was the first time she'd been close to a male friend since losing her brothers and she reveled in the difference that such a relationship could make. V.J. was currently single and shared with her the woes of dating in the gay culture, especially at his age, when so many men were devoted to long-time partners. He had no desire to seek out younger men.

Callie related to V.J.'s quandary because of her own

reluctance to take a dip in the dating pool. She found herself confessing her continued obsession with the unobtainable Jake. Even though she knew he was lost to her, she found herself idealizing him as the perfect man for her—someone she would never see or hear from again, but whom she could never find a replacement for.

Both of them warred with the stigmas attached to them—Callie with her physical and emotional scars, V.J. with his alternative lifestyle. They decided that they would be perfect for each other if only she was twenty years older and he wasn't gay.

V.J. waited four months before he invited Callie to become the display artist for all of his bookstores. Part of his success in business had been his objective decision-making and he didn't want his fondness for Callie to cloud his judgment about the work she was doing. The months of watching customer reactions to her displays and the sales numbers themselves convinced V.J. that Callie was indeed the prodigy she appeared to be.

Callie accepted her new role at the *V.J.'s* stores eagerly. Leah worked such long hours that Callie spent much of her free time accompanied just by the cat. She enjoyed the creative aspects of her display work more than the stocking. Traveling to all four stores meant that she would have time to do only displays. She and V.J. decided that she would spend one day per week, for nine hours, in each store, working her magic, peddling his wares as only she seemed to be able to do.

*C*allie's career was taking off and she grew more confident and busy. Leah was overjoyed to see Callie doing so well, but her own job was making her increasingly miserable. She loved sports medicine rehabilitation and she never regretted choosing *St. Katherine's* as the place to complete her training.

However, the long hours she worked and the late nights she studied cases were taking their toll physically. Leah grew thinner, her pep declining day by exhausting day. Callie tried to make sure her friend ate and that she took some time for TLC on her short weekends, but this grew harder as Callie worked more hours and spent more of her off-time socializing with V.J..

Leah admitted only to herself that part of her exhaustion came from her continued silent battle with Dr. Sean O'Carroll. She had spent many of her sleepless nights thinking about their brief conversation, furious with him for being so callous, even more furious with herself for being so unprofessional with him. She still noticed him at work, glancing at her from time to time, always looking away when she gave him a frank look in return.

She didn't work with him directly, so she couldn't figure out why he interrupted her thoughts so, why it bothered her so much that he refused to admit his interest. With just six months of fellowship left, she began to put out feelers for jobs around the city. She would be officially finished with her medical education. Her medical director at *St. Katherine's* wanted desperately to keep her there when she finished. She wanted to stay. She had worked hard for a position, in fact.

She couldn't help but wonder how miserable she would be, though, if she stayed and continued to be rebuffed by Sean O'Carroll.

She was in the cafeteria on a bleak February day when she decided to confess all to her colleagues at lunch and get their take on the situation.

Her regular group at lunch consisted of Jolynn, a third-year resident from Pediatrics, who had corkscrew blond curls and a dizzy personality to match; Mack, a thirty-year Radiology technologist who'd become a legend at *St. Katherine's* for his diverse imaging knowledge; Filipa, a gorgeous, curvy Latina occupational therapist from Leah's Rehab unit; Lanny, a native Texan who graced them with his cowboy demeanor on his breaks from the biomedical engineering department; and finally, Jake, a gentle giant from the Burn Center, who ate with them so he could flirt with Leah, Filipa, and Jolynn.

They were a varied bunch, but they all liked to talk—they had that in common—and they collectively knew almost all of the goings-on at *St. Katherine's*. Leah had joined the rest of them six months ago, noticing their lively table and gravitating to it one day, like she was always meant to be with them. They had been helpful informants regarding Dr. Sean O'Carroll and she had listened to them and they had dropped the subject, or so they thought.

Mack was the first to plunk his tray at their table next to Leah.

"Geez, Girl, you should add a few cups of bread pudding to that tray today. You look like crap."

"He's right, Leah," Filipa joined in, "You get any bonier and those scrubs are gonna fall straight to your knees the next time you reach overhead for a pillow from the linen cart."

"Thanks, guys. You look great too," Leah deadpanned. "I'm fine. I'm just a little tired lately."

"You should get that checked out," put in Jolynn as she sat down her keys and tray and sat with her left leg tucked under her bottom. "I just read in my newest Journal that fatigue and stress can be just an excuse young people use to cover up an eating disorder."

"I do not have an eating disorder, for Pete's sake, Jolynn," Leah defended, shoveling a spoonful of mashed potatoes home for effect.

"I'm just saying…" Jolynn reddened and turned to

her shrimp salad.

Jake and Lanny were the last to join them each displaying his own distinct swagger as they approached the table. "Hi Mack, Ladies," they said almost in unison.

Leah let out a brief snort, "You guys look like you just jumped out of a Marlboro ad. All you would need to do, Jake, is take off that white coat and stethoscope and those chinos would be screaming, 'Follow me, ladies.' Lanny, you're already way too fine in those *Wranglers*. How is it that you biomedical guys get to wear such sexy jeans?"

Lanny had the grace to blush. "Well, now, Miss Leah, I imagin' that crawlin' around on the floor tearin' apart Mack's lemon of an MRI, makes us qualified to dress down just a little. Jake's chinos would never hold up."

"Enough about my chinos. You'll notice that I'm keeping them covered for now." Jake sat down quietly and winked at each of the girls, charming them silently, as he always did.

Jolynn piped up. "We were just telling Leah that she needed to eat more. Isn't she starting to look a little scary underneath those scrubs?"

"You are lookin' a might bit angular, but I didn't wanna say nothin'." Lanny was always the gentleman.

"All right, already. I'll try to eat more!" Leah threw up her hands in surrender.

"Something bothering you?" Mack asked his question between healthy-sized bites of Salisbury steak.

"There is something I wanted to talk to you guys about," Leah confessed.

"Don't keep us in suspense," Filipa gave Leah her full attention.

"Dr. Winters offered me a job here last week. He's been impressed with me during my fellowship and he wants me to stay. It's a pretty sweet offer."

They let out a collective cheer. Not one of them had looked forward to Leah leaving their ranks.

Jake asked, "Why do I sense that this job offer is a problem for you?"

"I love you guys. You know I do. And I love my job here as well."

"But. There's always the big, old 'but,'" Jolynn offered.

"You're right, Jolynn. I'm still having a problem with Sean O'Carroll."

"Why that no good sonofagun, crankypants...."

"No, Lanny. It's not him. Yeah, he still checks me out once in a while when he doesn't think I'm looking. That's not the problem. He hasn't been inappropriate in any way. The problem is mine. I want him to notice me, to approach me, to ask me out."

"Why? Ew, he's like so old," Jolynn grimaced. "Sorry, Leah, but he is."

"I've looked at his hospital bio. If he finished school when it looks like he did, he would only be twelve years older than me. I don't know what it is, really. He's mysterious and he seems sort of lonely. He just intrigues me. He's good-looking and awesome at his job. Being older means that he's dignified, like he could be a gentleman."

"And we're so hard to come by these days," Jake offered with a twinkle in his eye. Leah gave him a playful swat and then her eyes softened.

"I know you had your heart broken last fall, Jake. Things changed after you got back from vacation. It's hard to move on, isn't it?"

"Indeed, Leah," was all he offered in response.

"I'm just not sure I could put up with Dr. O'Carroll's aloof attitude day in and day out, once I had a choice in the matter. I could end up severely disappointed."

"I can't disagree with you," Jake replied.

"Now wait just a minute," Filipa reasoned. "Maybe Dr. O'Carroll is keeping his distance because you're a student at *St. Katherine's*. That makes you strictly off-limits. If you were working here, you would be a colleague, a peer. You could say or do whatever you wanted to him then."

"And he could still break your heart," said Jake.

Leah hadn't thought of it that way. She would certainly never harass Sean O'Carroll if he rebuffed her efforts, but if she stuck around, she could at least tell him how she felt. Getting a job elsewhere would only make her wonder what might have been. She really did love this place, these people.

"I might have to take that risk, Jake. After all, where else could I find such a lively lunch crowd?"

They all smiled and moved their conversation onto a hotter topic—whether the OB nurse at table six was going to finally trip that good-looking resident she'd been fawning over for a week. As their forty-five minutes of fun continued, only Jake noticed the tears repeatedly threatening the corners of Leah's eyes. He could only hope that the high and mighty Sean O'Carroll didn't put more of them there.

Chapter 10

Kim Li awoke to the smell of sandalwood and opened her eyes to the riot of rich burgundy and emperor's gold that adorned her tiny room overlooking the bustling Chinatown district. Already, at six o'clock in the morning, the district prepared diligently for the day's onslaught of tourists and patrons. The garbage truck backing to the building next door provided the only alarm Kim ever needed.

She dressed quickly, saving her daily shower for the end of her work shift. The community bathroom at the end of the hall was always far too busy in the mornings for her to use.

Kim put her teapot on the hotplate to warm. She inhaled the scent of the ginseng tea leaves and took in the calm beauty of her abode. She would, as always, need to find her inner peace this morning before she went to work. She considered hers among the most grueling jobs of the district, but she worked hard to be assigned to the task she did every day.

Kim Li was a fortune cookie maker and she did it by hand, sometimes completing as many as ten thousand cookies in a day with just cookie irons and quick hands. She'd worked in the shop for fifteen years, peddling the cookies until she was deemed fast and knowledgeable enough to command the irons. She had earned a meager fifty dollars a day until she graduated into the most honorable job at the factory. Now she brought home more than one-hundred and fifty dollars per day.

She could afford to pay rent for a fancier room by now, but she spent her extra earnings surrounding herself in silken luxury instead. She also put money aside to send to her relatives in China and a little went into a fund that she hoped would buy her own Chinatown business one day.

Kim was just thirty-one years old and it was merely a year ago when she'd thought all of this luxury and good fortune had come to a painful end. Scalding of the fingers was a common occurrence when working with hot irons as she did each day, but Kim had never really had a serious burn. It was a clumsy stock boy who knocked a filled iron into Kim's lap that fateful day.

The hot batter and upset iron flew into her chest and abdomen and the blistering batter continued down her legs. She pushed the iron off of her lap quickly, preventing further bodily injury, but damaging the palms of her hands. The pain was excruciating, unlike any she'd ever felt, and she eventually swooned as she was overwhelmed with it.

It was Dr. Jake Lamb who came to her rescue. The most serious of burn cases in the wider San Francisco area were taken to *St. Katherine's Hospital*. Dr. Lamb was a premiere burn specialist and he had met Kim Li at the door, immediately taking in her serious wounds and applying the magic that would minimize the long-term damage.

Kim Li awakened to find a giant, sea-blue-eyed man leaning over her in concern. Her child-like stature and obviously devastating state of pain touched Dr. Jake and he set about trying to make her as comfortable as possible.

His gentle bedside manner soothed her, even as he and his team worked miracles with her second and third-degree burns. The smock she wore fended off some of the liquid heat that might have made her injuries worse and as she healed, they discovered just one area of injury just above her navel that would need an artificial skin graft.

Kim Li worried that she wouldn't be able to return to her job. Dr. Jake Lamb assured her that the care he took with her ever-valuable hands would insure that she would return to the factory after a few months of recovery and physical therapy. Her boss graciously kept her place at the factory open, since it was his bumbling nephew who injured her in the first place.

Kim Li grew to love Dr. Jake. She imagined almost every young woman he treated would fall for him, in a way. After all, for an American, he was gorgeous, with gentle blue eyes and hair the color of rich caramel. Kim often felt dwarfed by him, but never intimidated. He was a remarkable doctor and she sent thanks to the Gods once again as she left her small room and walked into the brilliant spring day that he was there to fix her so she could continue to do her important work.

*K*im Li was correct that Dr. Jake's female patients adored him, whether they were nine or ninety. He enjoyed the attention. The only woman who was a constant in his life was his aunt Felicia and, though they kept in touch, she was a world away from his life in San Francisco. He enjoyed female company and he'd been hesitant to date since Callie had stood him up. Maybe it was because his mother left he and his dad when he was so little. He didn't want to feel that sense of abandonment again.

Kim Li was in for a checkup and she noticed Dr. Jake brooding. "Why you so sad, Dr. Jake?"

"I'm sad because I'm not going to be seeing much more of you, Kim Li. Your burns are almost completely healed."

"That sweet, Dr. Jake, but I still bring fortune cookies, even when I work."

"I can't wait," he replied, patting Kim Li's shoulder warmly. He empathized with her injuries, the pain she must have felt. He was like that with all of his patients. His past, as much as he tried to forget it, demanded that he feel passionately about this specialty. Helping people was more than his job. It was his retribution.

"You pouting again, Dr. Jake." Kim Li teased.

"Well, if I'm honest, it's about a girl," he admitted.

"Lucky girl."

"She got away, though. But I'm moving on. She won't make me pout anymore."

"Good. I like you smile," Kim Li smiled and Jake couldn't help but smile back.

It was August and, after almost a year, it was time for Jake to move on. He and his loyal bloodhound, Bob, had a thoughtful discussion earlier that morning. Bob was worried about his reticent master and it was starting to show even as they played Frisbee in the park after work. Neither one of them put their heart into it and Bob finally put his ginger-colored chin on the ground and gazed longingly at Jake, refusing to play any further catching games.

Jake acknowledged Bob's admonition and he promised to do better. After all, he had a hot party to go to that night. His friend Leah was throwing a party on her apartment building rooftop to celebrate the official end to her medical school career. She was becoming a bonafide medical staff member at their hospital and she'd invited all of her work friends over.

Just to set Bob straight, he acknowledged that Leah wouldn't be a female to pursue since she also subtly invited the object of her romantic attentions to the party. Jake had every doubt that the man would show, but he wished Leah well in her endeavor.

As for him, he would try his best to be charming, flirtatious, gentlemanly, and if the night should end with a suitable female on his arm, he promised himself (and Bob) that he would get her number.

Jake dressed carefully for his night out, selecting a casual cotton button-up shirt that matched his eyes and donning Leah's favorite Chinos in a warm chocolate. He decided a rooftop barbecue was too relaxed for a tie, so he left that off and grabbed a pair of brown loafers and a braided belt to match. He even put on some of the cologne he'd picked up in Belize City, a subtle reminder of his trip, a richly spicy musk that a native island lady on Caye Caulker recommended to Jake. He hoped it would work some of its magic tonight.

He bid Bob goodnight and settled him into the utility room with his pillow, plenty of food and water, and a friendly scratch behind his ears. Bob wished him luck.

It was an arduous drive across town. Everyone in San Francisco looked for something to do on that balmy August Saturday evening. Jake only hoped that there would be open parking somewhere in Leah's neighborhood. One thing he detested about living in the city was the endless number of circles one made of a city block, waiting for someone to leave so that one could get parking reasonably close to his or her destination. He was used to it, but his small-town upbringing still meant it rankled him.

The evening had a little chill to it as he parked and walked the three blocks to Leah's building and he was glad he'd brought his suede blazer. He squeezed his imposing frame into Leah's entryway and rang the security buzzer. A man's voice answered.

"Yes?"

"I'm sorry, do I have the wrong apartment? I was

looking for Dr. Leah Westfield?"

"Oh, yes. You needn't have rung. Leah's had the door unlocked for the evening. I am a good friend of her roommate and I've only come down for a tray of appetizers. Please come on up."

It was only as he rang off, that Jake noticed the handwritten sign to the right of the doorway that invited the guests of the rooftop party to help themselves inside. He smiled. Obviously Leah wasn't worried about anybody crashing the party uninvited. She invited virtually everybody who approached the door inside!

V.J. Banks was just exiting Leah and Callie's apartment with two trays of finger sandwiches when Jake met up with him on his way to the roof.

"Can I help you with those?" Jake offered, seeing that the slender man was no waiter and that he would require help opening the door to the roof.

"Well, aren't you a robust young man? Of course, I would love your help," V.J. answered.

If there was one thing Jake was used to, it was the appreciation he drew from men of V.J.'s persuasion. San Franciscans were nothing, if not open-minded. He simply smiled, reddened a little, and took the trays from the effeminate man.

V.J. led the way down a wide hallway, opening the door to the rooftop and remarking along the way what a lovely party and what delightful friends Leah had. He pointed to a table to the left of the barbecue grill where Jake could set down the trays and it was precisely then that Jake almost dropped them.

There before him was an apparition, such that had come to him in many, many dreams, but never while he was wide-awake. It was his Callie. Callie of the White Sand. She was ethereal in her long-sleeved crimson sheath, secured at her slender waist by a mother-of-pearl conch belt. Her ebony locks cascaded gently past her shoulders and she appeared to be smiling at V.J. as he sidled over to her, her cat-like eyes glowing with the joy of the evening.

The trays bobbled and Jake managed to catch them as Leah hurried over and grabbed one from him.

"Hi Jake! Looks like V.J. put you to work on your way up," Leah remarked casually. Then she noticed that he was paying no attention. "Jake?"

"Sorry?" Jake replied, finally tearing his eyes away from Callie and paying a silent greeting to the guest of honor.

By then, though, Leah had read the direction of Jake's gaze. "You look like you just got run over by a Mac truck! She's gorgeous, isn't she? I think I need to introduce you to my roommate, Callie."

"Callie?" Jake replied weakly.

It was then that Callie finally stopped her musing with V.J. and Leah's friend, Scott Furlow, and noticed the roof's newest guest. She immediately dropped the only object she held. The plastic wine glass skittered across the concrete floor as Callie met Jake's dazed eyes. Then she did what her instinct told her to do. She ran. The party-goers could all only watch with curiosity and amazement as Callie slammed through the roof door with Dr. Jake Lamb hot on her heels.

Chapter 11

*I*t didn't take Jake's loafers long to overtake Callie's stilettos, though she was running as if her life depended on it.

Jake put his hand on her shoulder, and she whirled around to face him. They were in front of her apartment door. She weighed simply running in, slamming, and locking the door, but she'd forgotten how imposing and athletic Jake was. She probably wouldn't even make it one step further if he didn't want her to.

What Jake did next surprised both of them. Apparently he'd gotten past all of the anger and regret of the last year and he realized he was just overpoweringly happy to see her. Tears sprang to his eyes and he pulled Callie to his chest in relief. His chest rumbled as he spoke the words. "Callie? Oh, thank God. I thought I'd never see you again."

It felt so, so good to be in his powerful arms, but Callie pulled away.

"I didn't expect to see you either, Jake." As she spoke she looked behind him to notice that Leah and V.J. were looking on to make sure everything was all right.

She decided to break the spell and introduce their friends to the conversation. After all, she had no idea how to deal with Jake in person, now that she had so idealized him in her imagination. "Jake, you obviously know Leah, but I'd like to introduce you to my friend and employer, V.J. Banks."

The other two reluctantly joined them in the hallway.

V.J. reached for Jake's hand. "I didn't get a chance to introduce myself earlier. It's nice to meet you, Jake. I've, um, heard so much about you."

Callie's eyes met his in warning.

"I mean from Leah, of course," he lied weakly.

"It's nice to meet you, too," Jake replied tersely, but it was obvious by his concentration on Callie that he wished to speak with her privately.

"Callie, Mystery Man, if you're okay out here, I need V.J.'s help with the music." Leah grabbed V.J.'s hand and led him back toward the roof.

Callie pleaded with her eyes, but Leah knew that Jake would never harm her friend. V.J. wasn't so sure, but he let Leah lead him away, nonetheless.

Their exit led to a prolonged silence as each assessed the other, the year of absence and longing weighing heavily in the air between them.

"Can we talk, Callie?" Jake finally offered, gesturing to the apartment.

"I guess I owe you that much after standing you up, don't I?"

They entered the apartment and she took a place on the worn sofa, patting Beulah as she sat down. Jake didn't trust himself to sit on the sofa with her without wanting to touch her, so he seated himself on the wicker lounger across from her. It groaned under his bulk, but after a tense moment, took his weight.

"I want to ask you why you left," Jake began, "But first I want you to know how much I've missed you. We had only those two days together, but I felt like we made a powerful connection. Was I wrong?"

"No, Jake, you weren't. I felt it too. I might as well be honest with you."

"Please," Jake listened raptly.

"I bolted. I called up Leah and told her I was coming, I packed my things, and I ran away from the island."

"Because of me?"

"Because of what you represented. You were different from so many other people, Jake, in that I wanted to get to know you better. I wanted to let you in to my life, tell you everything, share my past. That is not an easy thing for me to do.

"It's taken the last year, getting to know Leah better, befriending V.J., that has taught me that my story isn't really shameful, as I always thought it was. It isn't painful to share myself with them, because they love me despite what I've been through and all of my baggage."

"So you were afraid to let me into your life?" Jake tried to sort through what she was telling him.

"I've never been romantically involved with anybody, Jake. Nobody."

He took this like a blow to the gut. He couldn't fathom how anybody as beautiful and intriguing as Callie could get this far into her life without ever having a relationship. It would be an awesome responsibility to be her first love. He also realized that he wanted to take that responsibility.

"I don't care about that, Callie. Do you realize that I haven't been able to get over you? My best friend, Bob, is beside himself trying to figure out how to help me. I've been hopeless for the last year." He rolled his eyes and silently pleaded with her to understand.

Callie laughed lightly. "You hardly seem hopeless. Do I get to meet this 'Bob' sometime? I'd like to set the record straight."

"Absolutely. He's a bloodhound and he's a real sucker for the ladies."

Callie giggled in earnest and she became serious once again.

"Can I ask you a favor, Jake?"

"Only if you promise me that you won't run away again."

"I promise. I was wondering if we could take this nice and slow this time."

"I'd like that, Callie. We could start by going back to Leah's party. Some of my other friends are here from the hospital and I'd like you to meet them."

"That sounds perfect. Just one more thing, though."

"What's that?" Jake asked, his curiosity piqued.

Rising from the sofa and linking her hand with his, Callie pulled Jake from his perch. Then she put her left hand on his cheek, softly kissed the other, and whispered in his ear. "I'm so glad you found me again."

"Me too," he whispered back. He pulled away and grinned.

"Can I ask you something?"

"What's that?" It was Callie's turn to be curious.

"Callie of the White Sand, what is your last name?"

"It's Justice."

"I'll say," he replied sardonically.

She chuckled and they made their way back down the hall to the party.

Chapter 12

*C*hinese lanterns in green, yellow, and orange hung from wire that Leah and Callie had strung the evening before from the corner posts of their stucco roof. Citronella candles of the same colors lined the centers of the tables and repelled any uninvited insects. Pots of white calla lilies decorated the railing and each of the tables. The night was surprisingly clear and the stars could be appreciated from the festive roof, adding to the celebratory mood of the party.

Leah's coworkers from *St. Katherine's* and friends from her stint at the DA's office and their spouses and guests stood among the tables, conversing and sipping wine and champagne from plastic flutes. V.J., seeing that most of Leah's guests were of the right age to appreciate it, had chosen eighties' music to act as the background for their animated conversations.

Mack, the master of radiology and diagnostic imaging, was also a master griller and he stood guard over the marinated chicken and tri-tip steaks that sizzled and spit on his huge gas barbecue. It had taken four men and nearly half an hour of sweat to get the grill to the rooftop the evening before, so Leah was doubly appreciative of smells that wafted tantalizingly through the air. She set a huge bowl of potato salad on the buffet table and returned to the line-up of coolers behind her to fish out a container of Caesar salad.

As she set out the rest of the feast, Leah's eyes kept

returning to the lovely flowers she'd placed at the main serving table. She smelled the white roses mingling with the aroma of food. Violet-colored orchids and coral bell blooms further brightened the arrangement. She wondered again at who might have sent them, for they arrived with no card. The delivery man left before she discovered the missing card.

Leah called the florist, but they were unable to find any information about the transaction either. She finally accepted the anonymity of the gift, figuring that one of her guests would comment upon them and confess his or her responsibility for them. After all, everybody she knew was at this party.

'Well, almost everybody,' she thought, the butterflies in her stomach beating their giant wings once again, as she thought about the invitation she'd extended to Sean O'Carroll just a few days before. Leah left the note atop the chart of the only inpatient he had at the hospital. She watched him open the envelope from her obscure location at the nurse's station. His back was to her, so she couldn't see the reaction on his face, but he hadn't thrown the note away. He put it carefully into the pocket of his lab coat.

Her eyes darted once again to the roof door as it opened. Would he come to help her celebrate, to break the ice between them, now that they were colleagues, on a level playing field?

Leah let her shoulders relax once more as Callie and Jake emerged through the doorway. Well, at least she knew Callie was okay, not that she'd had any doubts about Jake's intentions for her roommate. She marveled once again at the fact that Callie had been Jake's mystery woman from Belize. Leah had made the connection the minute Jake laid eyes on Callie. The absolute surprise and raw pain on his face as Callie fled had made it clear enough.

It truly was a small world. Maybe now he would quit moping, she thought wryly.

They looked happy. No, she thought, they actually looked giddy. That was the best way to describe it. Leah's heart warmed to the romance developing between two people she thought very highly of. If she felt a lightning quick pang of jealousy, she tucked it away just as quickly and silently wished them well.

V.J. was watching the door as well. He'd grown protective of his friend, Callie. By now he was her confidante and did she not know of his own escapades and indiscretions, he would have felt a might bit paternal where she was concerned. They knew way too much about each other to be anything but the best of friends. He would never tell a daughter the things he shared with Callie.

She looked ethereal tonight, all dressed in dark red. She was beautiful before Jake chased her off the roof. Now she was breathtaking, aglow with the attraction she obviously felt toward her new companion. V.J. was concerned for her safety, but he could see by the besotted look on Jake's face that he need not have worried.

That didn't mean that Jake was off the hook. V.J. made his way subtly their direction as they greeted Leah once again and all three of them laughed at the irony of Jake and Callie's reunion.

V.J. eyed Jake warily, sizing him up to see if he truly was good enough for his lovely friend. He was certainly a strapping young man and Leah mentioned that he was a doctor that she worked with. Both were plusses, but V.J. still had questions.

He approached, extending his hand to Jake in greeting.

"I don't believe our first introduction was proper—just a little dramatic, I think. I'm V.J.."

"Jake Lamb. It's nice to meet you, properly, this

time."

Callie joined in. "Jake, V.J. is my boss and my very good friend. He owns the *V.J.'s* chain of bookstores here in San Francisco."

"I'm familiar with the one in the Haight neighborhood. It's *Vexing Journeys*, isn't it? I've always thought that was a fetching name for a bookstore," Jake commented.

"Well, thank you. It's not so easy to create a name with initials like V.J. and it took me some time to think of four separate names. I'm not so bright in the creativity department. Just ask Callie. She's my idea person. I'm just a keen business man and a lover of all things written."

"You're too modest, V.J.," Callie chided gently. She smiled and touched V.J.'s arm affectionately. It was apparent to Jake that the two were close. It was also obvious that V.J. was very gay, which made the friendship entirely platonic. Jake was relieved to see that this man in her life would not be a threat. He just needed to win V.J. over and that would be easy, because he was genuinely enamored with Callie.

"He's created an empire," she continued as Jake admired the glint of the Chinese lanterns off her raven hair, trying mightily to concentrate on the conversation too. "That takes more than good business sense. I'm just doing my best to keep the ball rolling."

"What do you do for the bookstores, Callie?" Jake's interest was piqued. He realized suddenly how very little he knew about Callie. It had been nearly a year since he saw her and he only learned just a smidge about her then. Jake was eager to know more.

"I travel between all four of the stores setting up book displays."

"She's a genius," V.J. interjected proudly. "The books she decides to put on display fairly fly off the shelves. It's as if she makes them speak to my customers."

Jake laughed. "I called her 'Callie of the White Sand' while we were in Belize. Perhaps she brought a bit of good luck back with her from those white sand beaches."

"Or perhaps she's a goddess with a golden touch," V.J. teased.

"Or maybe she's a witch," Leah teased as she joined in the animated conversation.

"Hey!" Callie objected, laughing gaily. "I'm standing right here, you guys. I swear I'm not using any magic. I just like what I do and V.J. here gives me the freedom to do it well."

"I'll have to come see, Callie," Jake regarded Callie fondly.

V.J. still hadn't gotten his chance to size up Jake, though he seemed nice enough. It was time to ask some questions of his own.

"So, Jake, Leah tells me that you met Callie in Belize?"

"I did. Callie stumbled over me on one of those white sand beaches while she was on her morning walk."

"You make it sound like I tripped and that was it, Jake. I sprawled all over you. It was horrifying!" Callie turned red remembering the embarrassment of that moment.

Leah chuckled. "So your first meeting involved a roll in the sand? You never told me that, Callie."

"Well, it wasn't exactly one of my more graceful moments."

Not wanting to be rude, but wanting to know more, V.J. changed the subject.

"So, you're a doctor, Jake? I noticed you didn't introduce yourself as such when we met officially."

"You're a doctor?" Callie was fascinated. "I was

wondering how you knew Leah."

"I don't generally introduce myself as 'Dr.' when I meet new people for two reasons. First, my job, as much as I love it, isn't really who I am. I want people to know me before they know my chosen career. Second, it can be intimidating to a non-medical person to meet a doctor as opposed to a regular old guy named Jake."

"I can't believe we never talked about it," Callie marveled. "I've seen how hard Leah has to work to be a doctor. It must be important to you."

Leah interrupted. "Jake is like the rest of us. He loves his work, but he doesn't want it to suck up his entire identity. My guess is that, because you were on vacation and trying to get away from the stress of your job, that you just didn't see the need to mention it. Am I right, Jake?"

"That's exactly right, Leah. I would have told you more eventually, if you'd given me a chance," Jake smiled and winked at Callie. He could only do this now because he'd finally found her again. It was easier to make the rejection seem lighthearted.

"So do you work in Sports Medicine with our Leah?" V.J. was still sizing him up.

"No, my specialty is different. We're just lunch buddies, along with some of the other gang that's here. I specialize in treating severe burns."

Neither Jake nor V.J. noticed Callie blanche and subconsciously rub her arm through the fabric of her shirt. Only Leah knew the effect this revelation would have on her embattled friend. The irony of Jake's profession hadn't escaped Leah when it came to Callie. Leah knew more than anyone about Callie's scars. She only hoped that Jake's knowledge of burn treatment would make things better for Callie, not worse.

Seeing Callie's discomfort, Leah quickly changed the subject.

"Speaking of the gang, I haven't properly introduced V.J. to Mack, Jolynn, Lanny, and Filipa." She gestured toward the grill where the gang had joined Mack. "By the way, they're staring holes in all of us, I think I'd better introduce Jake's new amour, Callie, to them as well!"

Chapter 13

Leah sighed as she signed off the last of the charts she was reviewing. It had been a busy week between football and baseball injuries and hockey mishaps. Their patient load coincided with seasonal sports and Leah found fall to be the busiest time of year.

It wasn't like her to be so melancholy, especially in the fall. Sure, she missed the turning of the leaves that happened earlier and more dramatically in Washington State. When she was little, she and her moms would occasionally drive to the Eastern part of the State. In Chelan County, during apple harvest, there were breathtaking contrasts woven by gold and sienna-leaved apple trees meeting and reflecting off of the vast Columbia River.

Fall was beautiful in San Francisco as well, with the weather getting mildly cooler and the days shorter. Her neighborhood got a little foggier and the storefronts became more festive, pumpkins, scarecrows, and maple leaves multiplying each day. The usual city smog carried the faint scent of wood smoke as people began to use their fireplaces.

Halloween was just a few weeks away and she loved how her family-friendly neighborhood received the cute, tiny witches, ghosts and ghouls door to door, just as happily as the suburbs did. She and Callie were organizing a mini-haunted house for the foyer of their building, just for fun.

'I should be happy,' Leah thought. 'Callie and Jake are doing great—two of my closest friends, finding each other half a world away, losing each other, and then coming together again. What good fortune. And I have the job of my dreams and I love doing it every day. What is my problem?'

She knew what her problem was, but she'd be damned if she would admit it aloud. Dr. O'Carroll was still giving her the cold shoulder. He hadn't shown at her party and when they ran into each other at the hospital, he was cordial, but aloof. She needed a new obsession, because he obviously wasn't going to come around

Leah was lonely. Callie worked long days like Leah did, and when she wasn't working, Callie was spending time with Jake (though not overnight, Leah noticed.) It was good they were having fun together and Leah was glad they were taking things slow and getting it right this time. At first, Callie was cautious and a bit wary, but Leah could see that she was increasingly enthralled with Jake. Even V.J. seemed half in love with the guy.

Leah stopped her pondering long enough to go to the locker room and change her scrubs to gray wool trousers and an emerald green cashmere sweater. She smiled to herself. One thing she was taking pleasure in lately was shopping. It was nice to be making money again, finally. Thanks to help from her moms and student loans, she had lived comfortably for the last six years, but now she was actually making enough to start looking at the possibility of buying a house or condo in the spring. Leah was already saving for a down payment. Callie intended to keep the apartment if Leah moved.

Leah really did have a lot to be positive about. She slept better lately. She exercised and ate better, but she was still too thin. Her lunch crowd still wouldn't let her forget it either. They brought her a whole pumpkin cheesecake for dessert last week.

She had excellent friends and a charmed life, as she'd always had. Sister Ellen Ryan told her when she was a little girl that her luck must come from her shiny red hair. It was like a new penny. Sister Ellen was like a grandmother to Leah and she passed away the year Leah left Seattle. Leah really missed Sister Ellen. She missed her moms too.

She chided herself again for feeling sorry for herself. It was Friday. She was going to meet Filipa at Romeo's for happy hour and they were going to have a fabulous time. Maybe she would meet someone new, or not. Either way, it would be fun and she was looking forward to getting her mind off of Sean O'Carroll.

*C*allie and Jake were also going out for happy hour. The margaritas at *Padre's* beckoned. Jake picked Callie up a few minutes after his shift ended at the V.J.'s on Haight and they drove to his townhouse to park his car. *Padre's* was within walking distance and neither of them felt like hassling with parking on a clement, fall Friday night.

Both were invigorated by their walk and they enjoyed their conversation and meal, as usual. Jake, just as much of a gentleman as he had been in Belize, pulled out Callie's chair, and rose casually as she did when she excused herself to the powder room. Jake kept his word and didn't push Callie physically, though it was becoming increasingly obvious to both of them that their attraction would not be held at bay forever.

They exchanged heated looks over their fajitas as the spicy food and tequila did wonders for their libidos. Sparkles shot from her eyes like diamonds, as Callie wondered how luxurious Jake's chestnut curls would feel as she ran her fingers through them. Jake flushed with increasing desire. He had never felt such raw attraction for a woman. Callie was a goddess, he was sure, with as much power to make him laugh, as to light a fire within him. She was worth waiting for, but if his judgment was correct, she was growing as restless with waiting as he.

Callie was still nervous about revealing her physical flaws to this man. It terrified her that she let two men, if she counted V.J., into her life so easily in such a short time. Her heart was opened since her arrival in San Francisco. She now had people to care about, who cared about her in return. She was powerless to stop it.

It replayed in her frightened mind over and over, however, that the last two males that she cared about this much perished in a fire that she and she alone survived. Would this happiness be snatched away just as cruelly? Possibly it could, she thought, but she couldn't continue to avoid it. Her heart needed sanctuary and she'd begun to believe Jake was offering it.

Their fingers entwined as they exited the noisy restaurant where live music began in full swing. The night bustled, but they continued along in companionable silence. It was beautifully clear and crisp and the fall leaves whispered as their steps fell lightly upon them. They paused at Jake's doorstep. He looked deep into her eyes and caressed her cheek gently. She responded to the gentle touch with a smile. He moved as if to open the garage door to get the car.

"Wait, Jake," was all Callie said.

Jake was back in front of her in an instant, taking her in his arms. Somehow they got the door open and made their way up the stairs, never breaking their contact, even as Bob bayed his joyful greeting. The landing at the top of the staircase opened into a spacious dining and living area, with an arched window revealing a stainless steel and granite kitchen.

Jake swept Callie onto his comfy black leather sofa, too impatient to carry her up the final flight of steps to his master bedroom. They explored the depths of each other's mouths, pausing to nip at an ear or taste the hollow of the other's nape. Jake backed off for a moment to take a deep breath and go slower with Callie. He didn't want to frighten her this time. She reached for him again and Jake rubbed her arms through her chambray shirt. Unconsciously and totally against her will, Callie stiffened beneath his hands.

Jake's breath let out in a whoosh. He'd rushed her and as he saw the terror fill her eyes once again, Jake cursed himself inwardly for making the same mistake. He sat up at the end of the couch, at her feet.

Callie wanted to cry, but she knew she had to explain herself. She couldn't run again from Jake. He deserved the truth.

"I'm so sorry, Callie. I don't know what my problem is. I just get so carried away with you."

"You're not the only one, Jake. This isn't your problem. It's mine."

Jake looked up, obviously crestfallen and Callie couldn't help but feel retched for her reaction. This tender man would never hurt her. She was sure of that.

"Jake, I need to show you something," she began, knowing that showing him would be so much quicker than telling her entire, tragic story.

"I don't want to push you…" he began.

"No. I know. Just let me do this. I trust you, Jake, more than you know. I know that, with your job and all, you'll understand."

Jake sat mystified as she adeptly worked apart her pearl buttons. He barely dared to breathe as he imagined her torso being the lovely match for the creamy, now blushing skin of her face. What she revealed took his breath away entirely.

Callie's modest neckline fell away to reveal the edges of extensive skin grafting. The entire right side

of her torso and her arm still bore the web-like scars
of the most severe of all burns brought to his practice.
She'd had some laser treatments, he could tell, but there
was still an enormous amount of reconstruction to do.
What amazed him, as his clinician's mind analyzed her
scars, was that her face and neck had been so masterfully
repaired. She had obviously undertaken many years of
therapy to get as far as she was toward healing her burns.

Suddenly he understood that this was much more
than a physical impairment that Callie had. Her scars
went far deeper than her skin. He looked back into her
face and saw unchecked tears running down her cheeks.
His eyes softened as they encouraged her silently. He
kissed the tears away.

"Are you still in very much pain, Callie?"

"Not physically. Not really. I take an ibuprofen if I
get uncomfortable. It's mostly just numb. And so ugly,
Jake. You can say it, you know."

"Oh, Callie. Yes, those are awful burns and someday
I want you to tell me the entire story of how you got
them and what you've gone through to make them better,
but not now, Honey."

"You're not repulsed by them? I've gotten used to
seeing them, but I know they're horrid, and…"

"Shhh," Jake's voice soothed. He pushed Callie's
hair behind her ears. He looked into her eyes.

"You're breathtaking, Callie. I've thought that from
the moment you tackled me on that beach. This doesn't
change that. Now that I know you even better, your
beauty couldn't be dimmed even if you had a huge wart
arising from your cute little butt."

Callie giggled nervously.

"You're just saying that. Wait'll you get a load of
that wart."

By now they were both laughing, the tension broken
by their bantering. Callie relaxed. This was really going

to be okay. She never dreamed it would be this easy to show her flawed body to this man that she loved. Her eyes reflected her already deep feelings. Jake grew serious as he returned her sweet gaze. He felt it too.

"I love you, Callie."

"I love you too, Jake."

And, ignoring Bob, who had yet to be properly acknowledged and who gazed at them both pathetically, they took up where they had left off, allowing their passion to reign at last.

Chapter 14

*I*t was the month of crisp fall leaves and brisk air filled with the smell of burn piles and newly used chimneys. It was the beginning of a winter confinement that would be soul-wrenchingly interminable.

The prisoner stood before a board of five strangers, people who knew everything about his crime, but knew nothing, really of the multitude of his sins.

Did he feel remorse? 'I feel confined,' he thought and bowed his head and answered in the affirmative.

Was he sorry for killing a man of God when he burned down that church? 'I am most certainly sorry that I lost my freedom, my privacy, my family,' he thought, and he nodded solemnly once more.

They didn't ask him if he still wanted to start fires, if his mind whispered to him, 'Torch everything.' It was a good thing, too, because then they would have read the malice, the evil that lurked behind his humble posture and passive façade.

He was cool and he was smart. Would they fall for it? Did he want them to? Did he deserve mercy?

He nodded once again as they thanked him for his time.

Chapter 15

*N*ovember brought rain and more rain. The gloom was oppressive and Leah tried hard not to wallow, still, in her loneliness, though it was getting worse now that Callie was spending more nights with Jake. The two of them were getting increasingly closer and Jake even hinted a few times at lunch about a Christmas engagement. Leah was thrilled for them. She was also completely jealous of the two of them.

She ignored the rather green shade of envy and told herself that she would find the same happiness, someday.

For now, she was too busy to contemplate dating. Her department lost their chief resident to an unfortunate drunk-driving incident. He was the perpetrator and the hospital suspended him. Leah thought him rather boorish anyway, so she was glad to see him go, especially since he was obviously stupid enough to tie one on and get behind the wheel. To make up for his absence, she and another rehab doctor agreed to split an extra shift. This meant she was working fifteen hours in a day instead of ten.

The extra work was therapeutic. It took her mind off her boring personal life. It also meant very little time in her empty apartment.

Leah exited these days exhausted, but exhilarated, her mind distracted by the many and varied cases she was working on. She found little time to cook, so she frequented a café three doors from her apartment building on a nightly basis. She took the bus to her normal stop, dropped her bag at home and grabbed her daily newspaper, and walked to the bistro, where they now called her by name.

She'd lost track of how many days in a row it had rained, but she was definitely thankful for her galoshes that Wednesday evening when she sloshed from the bus to her apartment. She was starving and in a hurry as she threw her *St. Katherine's* bag on the couch and grabbed a plastic shopping bag to cover her paper. She patted Beulah absently as the cat meowed her greeting. Then she was on her way again.

It was common knowledge in her neighborhood that they were badly in need of better lighting on the street. It was such a quiet place that dimmer streetlights seemed fitting, though they proved hazardous when the fog and rain moved in. Leah was in such a rush that she paid little attention to the steps she was taking. After all, she'd traveled this route hundreds of times since she moved here. What she didn't account for was the sinkhole that had developed in the sidewalk as a result of the heavy rains.

The unfortunate misstep sent her right foot into a hole four inches deep and roughly the size of her boot. She lost her balance and felt a devastating snap as she plunged forward, unable to catch herself. She might not have been so badly hurt, except the charming wrought iron bench that adorned that section of sidewalk rose up to meet her as she fell.

Her temple exploded into a blinding white light of pain, as Leah's mind fled into the bliss of unconsciousness.

Leah's accident occurred very near her bus stop and it was only a matter of five minutes between her fall and the discovery of her badly injured body by a neighbor. He recognized the petite young doctor and had a fellow rider summon an ambulance. Since her *St. Katherine's* identification badge still hung about her neck, there was little indecision about which facility to take her to. She would be transported immediately to her own hospital.

Her coworkers rushed to help Leah as soon as she arrived. Mack's on-call tech called him in to help with her CAT scan and x-rays, since he knew she was a personal friend. She was stable, but the bench had given her a concussion, and both bones of her lower right leg were broken. It would be three full days before she would be completely conscious again. This would be a blessing for Leah.

Chapter 16

*M*ack knew that Leah had no family in town, so he got permission from the attending physician to call Leah's friends. His first call was to Jake. He knew Jake would be privy to Callie's whereabouts and they needed Callie to contact Leah's family.

Jake and Callie rushed to the hospital, only to find that their friend was already in surgery, having a rod put into her tibia bone in her lower leg. Jake inquired about the surgeon, concerned that Leah be given the best treatment. He wasn't sure whether to be apprehensive or thankful when he learned the surgeon was Dr. Sean O'Carroll himself. After all, Dr. O'Carroll was the best, but he knew Leah's rocky personal history with the crankypants doctor. Lord knew what she saw in him in the first place.

Jake was hardly an expert in neurology, but he talked the attending into letting him look at Leah's CAT Scan and what he saw was reassuring. It was clear she had a concussion, but she would recover quickly and there would be no permanent effects.

Callie called Leah's moms in Seattle. It was five short hours later, though it seemed like an eternity to them, when Shirley Foster and Eileen Westfield arrived at the hospital. Leah had been a gift to them, more than thirty years before. Her mother, a homeless teenager who had resided briefly in their apartment, left Leah when she was just eleven months old, to be raised by them. Sunny,

Leah's mother, chose to give her daughter a life better than one lived on the streets. Shirley took care of Leah daily while her mother was working. By the time Sunny left, Shirley was already like a mother to Leah and both she and Eileen were grateful for the spunky redheaded child they'd had the privilege to raise.

It was doubly rewarding for them because their first child, a little boy named Garrett, was ripped away from them by the ravages of leukemia. Leah healed them in so many ways. She was their pride and joy. They had contemplated moving to San Francisco many times to be closer to her, but their bookstore in Seattle was modestly successful, and they knew Leah enjoyed the independence the distance afforded her.

Now, as they watched their vulnerable daughter recover from her injuries, Shirley and Eileen grappled with guilt that they were so far away when it happened. V.J. reassured them and offered his old friends a place to stay while they were in town.

Callie hardly knew Eileen and Shirley, but she knew they did a wonderful job bringing Leah up. Her friend loved her moms as much as any child could. Callie often envied Leah's relationship with her parents. She, Shirley and Eileen found themselves often those first few days companionably watching for signs of improvement in Leah.

Shirley found that she was curious about this young woman who had befriended her daughter so many years ago. She knew that Leah met her while she was a legal intern in Seattle. She also knew that Callie's case was very high profile in the media when she sued her adoptive parents. Shirley was inquisitive of people in general, though her way of engaging them was unobtrusive.

"I've been meaning to thank you for calling us right away, Callie," Shirley murmured quietly.

"Of course. Leah would have called you herself, if she'd been able," Callie replied.

Shirley turned her warm, amber gaze toward her daughter. "I wonder when she's going to wake up. The doctors said she is being sedated for now to let her brain rest, but they've been lightening the sedation gradually. I can't wait to see her lovely blue eyes."

Eileen joined the conversation. "That would be reassuring, wouldn't it?"

Shirley nodded, regarding her long-time partner affectionately, and patting Eileen's hand. Callie observed the two women who had spent more than four decades together as partners. Shirley's face was still youthful with soft, round eyes and a warm smile, surrounded by a chestnut mane infused with plenty of light gray. She wore it long, curly, and carefree. Eileen's hair was completely bluish-white, with no trace of the black it had once been, and pixie cut. Her visage was much more serious, but her face was narrow, smooth and largely unlined. Eileen was outgoing and much more bold than Shirley, saying what she thought without checking herself. Shirley was the temperate one, who attracted people with very little effort, and buffered Eileen's audacity.

Shirley continued to engage Callie. "So, Callie, V.J. tells us that you've made yourself quite indispensable at the *V.J.'s* bookstores."

Callie smiled. V.J. never spared any compliment where she was concerned. He really was a dear man. "I suppose that I have. I know I have you to thank for connecting me with him in the first place."

"Oh, sure, but you have made yourself the success that you are. I'm just glad we could help V.J. out. He's a very old friend," Shirley replied.

"He may have even fathered our first child, Garrett," Eileen added.

Callie raised her eyebrows. "May have? I'm not sure I understand."

"Well, that is certainly water under the bridge, isn't it, Eileen?" Shirley looked a little uncomfortable to be talking about the subject.

"Let me explain," Eileen replied, amused. "Shirley and I had a little boy named Garrett with an anonymous sperm donor among our gay friends here in San Francisco. V.J. was one of the donors. It really was forever ago. We lost Garrett to cancer when he was only eight years old. Time really doesn't dim the pain of losing a child, Callie. We really were just going through the motions of life when Leah was literally dropped in our laps. She has been the hugest blessing."

"Now that I agree with," Shirley said.

"She's been a blessing to me also, Eileen," Callie added softly, regarding her eerily silent friend once again as she lay dwarfed by her hospital bed.

"How so, child?" Shirley asked.

"I really had nowhere else to go when I came here. It's only been a little over a year and I feel like I have a family now. I was five years old the last time I felt that way."

"I'm relieved to know that Leah has developed such friendships away from her home. She loves you too, you know," Shirley replied warmly.

"I know. I've been so busy lately, though, with my new love interest. You met Jake. He's wonderful, but I feel like I've neglected Leah. I can't wait until she gets better so that I can tell her how much she means to me."

"I'm pretty sure that she can hear you now," Eileen said. "The doctor said she might be able to, though how much she'll remember, we don't know."

"I've been wondering, Callie, if you don't mind my asking," Shirley inquired gently. "You say that you had nowhere else to go when you came here. Do you keep in touch with your adoptive family at all anymore?"

Callie shifted uncomfortably. She hadn't talked about the Justices in ages. Of course Shirley and Eileen would know about them, though, because of the media frenzy that surrounded her case against them.

"They didn't want to keep in touch. Constance, especially, was very angry with me. My attorneys took care of any correspondence that needed to happen with them. I haven't seen or talked to either one of them for years."

"You don't know then…" Shirley began.

"Don't know what?" Callie asked, curious, as always, about the people who raised her.

"Oh dear, I'm not sure you'll want to know," Shirley clammed up.

"I'll tell her. She has a right to know, even if she doesn't keep in touch with them. It's been all over the news in Seattle," said Eileen.

"The Justices have been back in the news?" Callie asked.

"This may be upsetting to you," Eileen tried to be a little more like Shirley and soften the blow. "Constance Justice was killed just a few weeks ago in an apparent crime of passion by her long-time physician."

"That's awful! What is Cyrus going to do? He relied on his wife for everything, from pressing his clothes, to telling him which social events to attend, to informing him what his favorite foods were. I've never seen a man more dependent on his wife," Callie felt briefly sorry for her adoptive father. He would be completely alone in the world without Constance. She knew what that was like.

"You don't seem to be concerned for her. After all, she was killed rather violently. From what I read, he shot her and then himself after a confrontation that involved the entire clinic," Eileen added.

"Constance was a self-centered, manipulative,

controlling woman and she probably pushed the good doctor into doing what he did. I've always thought that most of the cruelty done to me was her idea."

"I'm just sorry you had to learn about her demise from us," Shirley apologized.

"Better from you than from some lunatic reporter who's tracked me down to find out my opinion."

"I'm surprised that hasn't happened yet, actually," Eileen put in.

"What hasn't happened?" Jake interrupted, his deep timbre coming from the doorway where he'd just heard the end of the ladies' conversation.

"Well, hello Jake," Shirley greeted her daughter's friend affectionately, ignoring his question.

"We were just talking girl talk, that's all, Jake," Callie offered. She would fill him in on the rest later. Jake knew very little about the people who raised Callie. She had yet to share everything with him, though she intended to tell him all about her traumatic childhood eventually.

"Well, I hate to interrupt your conversation, but Dr. O'Carroll asked the best way to clear the room so that he could examine his patient. I volunteered to let you all know."

"Oh, of course," Shirley stood and patted Jake's arm. "Eileen and I are badly in need of some coffee anyway. Can't seem to shake this fatigue since we traveled down here."

"I don't imagine you've been sleeping very well," Jake understood their worry for Leah.

"I know we'll all be so relieved when she wakes up," Callie stood with the other women.

"Can I get you a coffee too, Callie? I know you haven't slept a wink since Mack called you," Jake offered.

"That's sweet, Jake, really, but I need to make a

phone call, actually. Can I take a rain check?"

"Anytime, gorgeous," Jake smiled into her stunning, but tired green eyes. He glimpsed sadness. He supposed that could be for Leah. But there was something else, also. Fear?

Callie wasn't telling him everything. Thanks to his upbringing, Jake could spot a liar anywhere. He knew he and Callie had yet to scratch the surface of the bad things that happened to her when she was a little girl. He knew she was burned in a house fire and that she lost her family on the same tragic night.. But there were more gaps to be filled in. She hid something from him now.

He contemplated her seriously for a moment. They were building something remarkable between them and he trusted that she would tell him when she knew the moment was right. The last thing he wanted to do was push her away.

"Okay, ladies. Let's give the illustrious Dr. O'Carroll his space." He and Callie rolled their eyes, knowing the paces the doctor had put Leah through before her accident. They followed Eileen and Shirley out the door.

Chapter 17

*T*he weight on her eyes pressed her lids against her corneas like window clings. Still, Leah could hear voices. They were good voices. People she loved were talking about her. Then the voices faded. Silence again. Someone was here, though. She felt a light caress on her cheek, a tug on her wrist, and then pain. Sharp. But not in her head this time. Lower. Her leg.

Leah wanted to tell the person to stop. Better to leave the pain alone. She just couldn't form the words. She furrowed her brow in concentration. Willed her eyes to open.

And open they did. The room was instantly too bright and she closed them quickly again. She was awakening, though, and tried to open them again only more slowly. Blinking away the light. Trying to clear the cobwebs.

When she finally could see well enough to focus on the overhead light and realized, out of familiarity, that she was in the hospital, her hospital, Leah looked around. What she saw filled her heart and slowed its jogging beat all at once.

Sean O'Carroll was regarding her frankly, grave concern on his face. He looked like he hadn't slept in days. If Leah didn't know any better, she'd think he was actually worried about her. She looked to his right, toward the head of the bed. White roses infused with purple orchids and coralbells. She returned her gaze to

Dr. O'Carroll.

"From you? Flowers?"

"Shh, Leah. You've just awakened. You mustn't waste energy talking."

She implored with her eyes.

"Yes. The flowers are from me."

"Party, too?"

"I sent those too. I couldn't come, Leah. I didn't have the courage.

Leah had no words. She was inexplicably angry with this man, but grateful that it was Sean she woke up to.

"What happened?" Leah examined her thickly bandaged foot and felt the turban tightened about her head.

"You tripped on a large rut in the sidewalk and hit your head on a wrought iron bench. You broke your right leg rather badly in the process. I fixed it for you."

"You operated on me?"

"I couldn't let anyone else do it, Leah. I had to make sure it was done right."

Leah was fully awake by now, though her mind was as exhausted as her body felt beaten.

"Why would you care, Dr. O'Carroll?" She was so tired of fighting this man and her feelings for him. It taxed her already muddled brain.

"I do care, Leah. That's the problem. I realize that I have a lot of explaining to do, but I want you to rest for now. Let's just say that I was trying not to complicate either one of our lives. It's taken seeing you gravely injured to jolt me into realizing that I've been a fool."

"I'm awake and I don't need to rest, Dr. O'Carroll."

"You do, though, Leah. Please call me Sean. I was wrong to push you away. You were right all along. I have noticed you. You occupy my every waking thought and it makes it damned hard to concentrate."

"I feel the same about you, Sean. Why is it so hard to get you off my mind? I'm pretty sure I even thought of you while I was unconscious."

"We're going to explore that. I promise. As your doctor, though, Leah, I must insist that you rest your brain right now. I'll let your family and friends know that you've awakened. They're a diverse group, aren't they?"

Leah smiled softly. Yes, between her hospital friends, Callie and V.J., and her moms, the term diverse was putting it mildly; but she loved them all, and she had felt them with her, encouraging her to heal.

"I'll instruct the nurses to add another pain medication to your regimen since you'll be awake more now and I don't want you uncomfortable while you're moving around," Sean added. "I'll check on you again in a few hours. We'll talk later. Please do close those beautiful blue eyes. You need to rest so you can heal."

Leah was happy to comply because her heavy lids were about to slap themselves shut anyway.

*C*allie hung up the phone for the fifth time, cursing softly, evoking a mew from Beulah, whose intelligent eyes followed her about the living room.

Callie patted the wanton feline absently.

"Why can't I do it, girl? I should call Cyrus, express my condolences. I'm just not sure how I say, 'Hi, it's your long lost daughter. Heard your old bitch of a wife got waxed. I'm sorry, but good riddance?'"

Beulah purred and mewed again quizzically.

Callie chuckled lightly. "You don't care, do you, Beulah? As long as we talk to you and pat you, your world is squared away. I bet you wish you had a few mice to chase in this lonely old apartment, though, don't you? Maybe I should take you over to Jake's, so you can meet Bob. He'd keep you busy, I'm sure."

She continued to scratch Beulah's velvety ears. It was easier to talk to the cat than to face down the telephone once again.

Maybe she would write a letter to Cyrus, accompanied by a sympathy card. That would give away her whereabouts, but that didn't matter. Cyrus would be too timid to stalk her. His emotions during the trial and afterward had tended mostly toward regret. He had never said so, but Callie was pretty sure he'd never meant her any harm. His chief crime was neglect, and subservience to an evil spouse.

Far beyond grief and anger now, perhaps Callie's biggest hang-up was the unanswered questions that hung between she and her adoptive parents. She would never understand why they couldn't just love her and treat her like the traumatized child that she was. Was she so unlovable? Was there some flaw in her that made it impossible for them to care enough to get her the treatment she needed?

Or was it pure greed that drove the Justices?

She wished she could confide in Jake about the whole ordeal. He would know what to do. Her psyche alone could use the reassurance his searing touch and hungry gaze instilled in her. Still, as surely as she'd thought her mistrust of men, and people in general, had to do with her physical scars, hearing about Constance Justice's demise clobbered that idea. The woman had made her feel unworthy in every respect.

As much as she knew in her heart that she loved Jake, some force larger than herself coerced her to believe that he would never truly love her. It wasn't possible, because if a forlorn, orphaned, and critically injured five-year-old couldn't capture someone's love and attention, then the adult version could certainly do no better.

Tears began to fall, soaking her silken tunic, mirroring the deluge outside the apartment windows. The rain still hadn't abated since Leah's accident. Callie wondered at the soaked San Francisco landscape, leaning into the window frame for support. It made no sense that her surroundings should be so cleansed, when her core, dry as a parched desert floor, was shattering into thousands of grains of insubstantial sand.

Chapter 18

Leah came home to an apartment bursting with Christmas cheer. V.J. and Callie used the leftover red, green, and silver tulle and cheerful holly berries from the decoration of the *V.J.'s.* stores. They'd strewn them about until every countertop and doorway in the apartment was donned in Christmas cheer. Callie bought a small fiberoptic tree with dazzling white lights to put on the sofa table.

The scent of cranberry cider clung to the air as Leah maneuvered her cast behind the coffee table and plopped on the couch. Her mothers bustled about settling her hospital accoutrements to their proper places, while Callie brought her a teacake and cider. She relished the feel of her own worn leather sofa and the velveteen softness of the ever-present Beulah, who parked herself on Leah's lap just seconds after she sat down.

It was the last week of November. Thanksgiving passed with the whole turkey drill, served up on a chartreuse tray and covered by a blurred plastic dome. At least she was able to eat it on her own power. After all, with the bump she'd received to her head, she could well have been getting nourishment through a tube by then. She was, by all accounts, lucky to be hobbling about on crutches and spending the looming Christmas season recuperating at home.

She would have to do her Christmas shopping via *QVC*, though. The skies had finally cleared for a few days, but she had strict orders from Sean to confine herself to her apartment for at least three more weeks. The rod in her tibia made it more stable than most breaks at this point, but the bone next to it also needed to heal, so staying off of it was essential. As a sports medicine specialist, she knew better than anybody the detriment that could be done from defying doctors' orders. She would follow Sean's instructions.

He would know if she didn't anyway. Where Sean O'Carroll had been enigmatic and distant in the past, he was now attentive, sweet even. She'd begun to glimpse the warmth, the depth of caring, that his patients raved about. While he hadn't completely let down his guard, Leah had seen the flood of his regret in each gentle touch, in every thoughtful word.

She was more than Sean O'Carroll's patient. They were both unfurling, opening themselves, finally, to the possibilities. In fact, they had a date on Saturday. He was bringing the Chinese food and movies. Callie had already volunteered to get lost.

Leah was in more pain than she'd ever felt in her life, shirking the more powerful painkillers for their muddling of her already-injured brain, and favoring Ibuprofen. The pain was okay, though, because it convinced her that all of the other good fortune she was having was real. She was home and she had her good friends and her family close. She had survived and the man of her dreams had finally admitted that she occupied his dreams too.

She sighed with contentment as she grabbed the TV control and propped her leg up on the end of the sofa. Maybe *Regis & Kelly* would be entertaining. They had a guest chef preparing holiday recipes. As Callie departed with V.J. to return to work and her moms retreated to the dining area to play a low-key game of cards, Leah dozed and dreamed of vanilla lattes and gingersnaps and tasting them on the mouth of a sexy, hazel-orbed doctor.

V.J. rarely drove, preferring to stroll the San Francisco streets in all of their beauty and variety. When necessary, he often took taxis or buses to within a few blocks of his destination and walked the remainder of the way. It kept him slim and invigorated. On days like today, though, when he needed to transport himself and Callie across the city to his North Beach *Velour Jackets* bookstore, he took his diesel bio-fueled Mercedes.

Its pearly white profile purred over the streets, whisking he and Callie to an important meeting with his new manager, an intelligent, but unfortunate former beatnik who was resistant to allowing someone beside himself any creative control of the store. Callie was a genius, of this V.J. was sure, and he needed to cajole his new manager into believing the same. He truly believed that everybody could learn to work together, given the right communication, and, ah, persuasion. He hated the unpleasantness of letting anybody go. Callie would never be a casualty, but he wasn't sure about Ricky Mankas, his manager.

Still, Callie seemed ill at ease. He'd been used to withdrawn behavior from her before, but now they were friends. He tried to reassure her.

"You know, dear, you needn't worry so about Ricky. He'll come around to my way of thinking."

Callie had been lost in her own thoughts. She only heard part of V.J.'s comment and roused herself into the conversation.

"I'm sorry, V.J.. What did you say?" Callie replied.

"I said not to worry so about Ricky. You're really distracted, aren't you? Is it about Leah?"

"No. I'm finally convinced that she's going to be okay. Better than okay, actually. Did you see the way her doctor was looking at her when she left?"

"I did notice that, yes. Sparks were flying. I felt like ducking for cover. Am I to assume that he's the enigmatic doctor she's been fawning over all of these months?"

"Sean O'Carroll is one and the same. After the misery he's put her through, I wish I could say I don't like him, but he really is an okay guy. Pretty serious about his job, but that's a good thing when you're a physician, I think."

V.J. sensed that Callie was trying to divert attention from herself. As he steered the Mercedes onto a steep, narrow one-way street, he tried again to glean information from her.

"Well if it's not Leah on your mind, then you must tell me, Callie. Is it Jake? Oh dear, please do tell me that everything is all right with Jake. He's a catch, honey, and if you don't want him, then give me a shot."

Looking away from the breathtaking sparkle of the Bay as they crested the hill, Callie laughed. "Oh, I'm sure that's exactly what Jake would want, V.J.! He does prefer blondes. He told me that he's only ever dated blondes before. Don't go looking to snatch my man, though. It took me too long to find him again."

"That's a relief, but don't keep me in suspense, Callie. If it's not Leah or Jake that has you all awash in your pretty mind, ignoring me entirely, then I demand to know what you're thinking about."

"Oh, V.J.. I've been keeping this to myself, just because it's so complicated. I've told you and Leah more than anyone about the Justices, so I suppose you will understand. Eileen and Shirley told me that Constance Justice has died."

V.J. mulled over the news for a moment, then asked, "Was it quick and painless, at least?"

"It was violent, actually. She was gunned down by a

doctor whom she'd been blackmailing."

"Oh, that is messy. Are you feeling guilty because it's a good riddance, as far as you're concerned?" V.J. knew that this woman had never been kind to Callie, not like a mother should be at all.

"It is that. I also feel the need to contact Cyrus Justice and make sure that he's okay. Why should I even care?"

"Maybe because Cyrus Justice is the closest thing you have a to a living parent."

"Is history that important? He wasn't much of a parent," Callie replied.

"Granted, the Justices did terrible things to you, but you bear their name. All parents make mistakes. Look at mine. My mother, rest her soul, bought me a silk kimono in pink when she found out I was gay, as if my sexual preference equated to being a woman and having a woman's taste for clothing. My father started taking me to every *49ers* and *Giants* game he could get tickets for, hoping that by bathing me in testosterone and *Bud Light*, he could persuade me otherwise. I was twenty-two and barely out of the closet. They never did 'get' me and I stopped trying to make them. They died unhappy and confused about their only son. I've never shaken the guilt, either."

"Do you ever wish you could just ask them why? Why didn't they understand you? Why couldn't they love and accept you as a gay man?"

"I wish I had, Callie. They died of heart attacks within two years of each other, smokers, both of them. I couldn't tolerate it myself," V.J. waved his graceful hand as if to wave away the smoke-laden air of his childhood. "Anyway, I didn't ask those questions. I was afraid to, honestly, and I resented them and their ignorant assumptions.

"I'd understand if you hadn't the courage to call

your father," V.J. concluded.

"He's not my father, V.J.. He never was. My father was a kind, country gentleman and a tragic fire took him away from me when I was too young to understand, but too old to forget him."

"But you do have questions. Am I right?"

"I do."

"I'm not exactly one to give advice. After all, I've made so many of my own mistakes, how could I rightfully advise anyone?"

"You know I value your opinion, V.J.. You're one of my best friends. Please tell me what you think," Callie begged.

They arrived at *Velour Jackets*, a parking spot miraculously opening just a space away from the storefront as they drove up. V.J. maneuvered expertly into the space, killing his engine, turning to face Callie, and seeing the doubt clouding her expressive verdant eyes.

"You are free to do whatever you need, Callie, my dear. If you need to go away for a week or two, we will manage in your absence. Our displays will just stay put a little longer than usual," V.J. smiled and reassured her.

He continued. "I want you to be free from all of your demons. You have suffered enough and now with Jake you've every chance to be truly happy. I know something is holding you back from embracing your chance. These people who raised you fractured your spirit. Jake, Leah, and I are trying to mend it. If talking to Cyrus Justice will help with this, then you must speak to him. Do it in person, if that makes it easier. Get answers to your questions, Callie, and then come back to us healed."

V.J. patted her on the head, exited the car, and came around to her side to open her door for her.

Callie could see that her new nemesis, Ricky

Mankas, was watching through the shop window, so she gave him a little wave and a smile, then she turned to V.J. and kissed him fully on the mouth. If there was any doubt how this little meeting with Ricky would go, she quickly erased it. V.J. would side with her. They would get this over with and then she would be free to decide what to do.

She wondered how quickly and cheaply she could get a round-trip ticket to Seattle.

Chapter 19

Bob, the bloodhound, was familiar with long faces, after all, his own visage suffered from enough downward pull to impair a good drink from the toilet. He'd seen enough scowls on the face of his person, Jake, in the last year to satisfy his quota for a lifetime. Jake had been happier lately and that always translated into more treats and Frisbee time for Bob, too. Besides, he kind of liked his new girl. She scratched him just right on the spot between his jowls and his ears. She was a keeper.

Now, though, his owner's face was down again. Bob fixed him with his 'tell your best friend in the world the whole story' expression. If Jake was feeling better after conversing with him, he was sure to give him canned food instead of the boring dry stuff.

To Bob's relief, Jake fell for it.

"You're right, Bob. It can't be all that bad, can it? Just because Callie left without telling me why doesn't mean she's gone for good. She still likes us. Doesn't she, Buddy? How could she not?"

Bob rested his chin on Jake's lap and stared out the tops of his eyes into his owner's soul. *Who could help but love a face like Bob's?* Jake thought once again. *But she might not care so much for mine.*

Jake scratched his dog absently, trying to think of a reasonable explanation for Callie's behavior, as of late. Leah had been hurt badly and Callie had expressed her guilt about not spending enough time with her friend and roommate, but now that Leah was home, Callie had left suddenly on an unexpected trip. It made no sense.

Nor did it make sense that she'd been reserved around him since Leah's third day in the hospital. Something was bothering her. This he knew, but she refused to tell him and he refused to pry, not wanting to bruise the oh-so-delicate flesh of their budding relationship.

He had relished their pairing since they'd reunited in August—not only was she intelligent and fun-loving, she was sensitive and considerate. Though her scent and spirit always lingered, his townhouse never suffered for having an extra occupant. She always hung her bath towels on their rack, folded her clothing neatly and picked up her shoes. She cooked elaborate meals for the two of them and never complained as she joined him to clean up the mess afterward.

Callie loved on his dog, Bob, like he was her child, talking to him like the human that Bob thought he was.

And she was delicious. Oh yes, there was that. His loins tightened as he thought of the ardor and abandonment she'd displayed when they made love. Even that had been frustratingly hindered by her latest reserve.

Didn't she know that he wanted her here always? He was ready to ask her to move in. He wasn't sure yet, though, if she was ready to do so. Still, he'd been planning to ask in the next few months.

Then suddenly, the Sunday after Leah returned home, she'd left him a note in his drop box outside his front door. It read:

Dear Jake:

You will be terribly upset with me for

missing our dinner date and bowling tonight.
After all it has kind of become tradition, hasn't
it? Don't be too hard on me, because I have
to go. I have some pressing business from my
'former' life in Seattle. I'm going to see Cyrus
Justice, my adoptive father.

I also promised Bob a walk in the park
today, so you'll give him my apologies and a
sausage, won't you?

I'll be back soon, Jake. Don't worry.

Yours-
Callie

The letter had been so cryptically simple and light-
hearted. She was just going on a trip. No big deal. She
was planning to come back and she didn't want him to
worry. He didn't know why then, it weighed so much on
him that she was gone. He just couldn't shake the feeling
in the pit of his stomach that she was never coming back.

His attention turned back to Bob as his bloodhound
whined his concern for his owner. Bob felt it too. He
patted his friend, trying to reassure him, giving him a
can of beef gravy chow, and telling him that everything
was going to be all right. He tried hard to believe it also.

*C*allie hadn't driven in so long, that she knew it
would be foolish to navigate the Interstate 5 route from
the Sea-Tac Airport to Cyrus Justice's Redmond home.
She took a cab instead. It was surprisingly easy to get
Cyrus' address. She just 'Googled' him and got his
phone number and address.

The Justices had moved since her lawsuit—they
couldn't afford to maintain and pay taxes on the home
Callie had grown up in when she had stripped them of

most of their worth. Plus, they had faced prosecution for insurance fraud shortly thereafter, eating up whatever remained in legal fees. The two had never gone to jail, but they'd done umpteen hundred hours of community service and they had lost their home and their professional reputations. Still, Callie felt hardly vindicated. It was all just too tragic to feel any joy for their misery.

She arrived at the house at 3 o'clock. The winter gray of the Seattle skies had already begun to deepen into twilight. She had forgotten how early daylight waned in the Northern part of the States during the winter. The melancholy hue surrounded the simple white cottage before her and cast it in a shroud.

It was as if the pall of death had come over the house. Callie shuddered.

She climbed the steps and pressed the doorbell. Callie was not sure what she expected of the man she hadn't seen for eight years. But she wasn't prepared for the shell of Cyrus Justice. His ash blond hair was infused with shades of gray. His disarming chocolate eyes sung out his grief and his once serious and slender visage had fallen victim to gravity and stress. He'd grown jowls. He now bore a closer resemblance to a basset hound than to the distinguished man she remembered.

His somber expression changed to surprise at the sight of Callie. She was taken aback to realize that Cyrus was glad to see her. He stopped himself short of reaching to embrace her. Too much had passed between them to initiate familiarity.

"Callie. It's so good to see you. Your face is so...."

"Healed? Surgically corrected?" Callie interrupted, surprised to hear the bitterness in her own voice. She quickly put it in check when she saw the wounded submission on Cyrus' face. This wasn't what she was here for.

"I'm sorry, Cyrus. Yes, I have been put back together quite well. Sometimes, in fact, I hardly recognize myself."

"You're beautiful, all grown up. And your eyes haven't changed, Callie. I'd recognize you anywhere." Cyrus shifted awkwardly, unsure, and they briefly sized each other up, she on his tiny porch leaning against the screen door, and he standing in the open doorway, his arm still holding the door as if he was still deciding whether to let Callie in.

Callie finally broke the silence. "Can I come in?"

Cyrus' reverie dissipated and he realized he'd forgotten his manners. "Oh. Of course. Please come in." He stepped out of the way and allowed Callie through, directly into his front room.

Callie tried to be discreet about assessing the little house, but it was difficult to hide her dismay. The foyer in their old house had opened up to a vaulted sitting room with a towering rock fireplace and a view from the upstairs balcony, all facing floor to ceiling windows which gazed out toward Lake Washington. It had rivaled a grand ski lodge in its splendor.

The living room of this house was miniscule, the dual recliners and twenty-inch television eating up the bulk of the space. An arched doorway led to the other part of the house, which was obscured to her view. The place was neater than she had expected, but then Constance had always been the careless one, tossing her shawls and evening shoes wherever they might land. She recalled Cyrus being frequently compelled to pick up in the wake of his wife's untidiness.

Cyrus Justice obviously lived very simply these days. She did this to them. Callie didn't know whether to feel sorry or not. The home she grew up in was spacious enough for them to avoid her almost entirely, but it was lovely and she, like most grown-ups, had a whimsical attachment to the place that witnessed her childhood.

"It is very different from our other home, isn't it?" He offered.

"At least you have a roof over your head and it's tidy," Callie replied feebly, knowing that she possessed most of the money that could have kept them from this lifestyle.

"It's fine. Especially now that it's just me. I would have rattled about by myself in the old house anyway. Constance and I rented this five years ago, after spending the time between in apartments. I've gotten used to it. You mustn't feel guilty, you know."

This was the heart of it, Callie knew. She did feel guilty for doing this to the only parents she had.

"You did the right thing getting help for yourself, Callie. I can't speak for poor Constance, rest her soul, because she never did stop railing against the system that 'robbed' us of everything; but I never blamed you. We treated you badly. Your pain and suffering, well, I can hardly live with myself knowing what we did to you."

Callie's eyes filled with tears and she felt like a slighted thirteen-year-old once again. She sat with sudden resignation in one of the recliners.

Cyrus perched opposite her, his brown eyes sympathetic, pleading. "You haven't forgiven us, have you?"

"I didn't come here to reopen old wounds, Cyrus."

"You used to call me 'Daddy.'"

Callie swallowed a sob. She thought she'd come past this desire for parental attachment. But, God help her, she still wanted Cyrus to love her.

"I can't," was all she could manage to squeak.

Cyrus was crying by now also, gracefully, silently. He knelt in front of Callie and took her icy hands into his.

"You can call me Daddy. I know I don't deserve to

be anything to you. I would like to tell you that it was all Constance's fault, but that wouldn't be fair. Yes, it was her idea to start making claims for medical expenses. Money had gotten tight with our mortgage and her shopping habits and she talked me into the scam, just as she talked Doctor Koepke into the scheme that took her life. I went along, though, Callie. I'm responsible for that."

"You loved her."

"I loved you too."

"Then how could you?" Callie wanted to know the answer.

"We have so much to talk about," Cyrus rose from the shag carpet and wiped his elegant hands, doctor's hands, Callie remembered, on his slacks. "I was just about to make some herbal tea and munch on shortbread cookies and grapes. Will you join me, Callie?"

Callie grabbed a tissue from the side table and dabbed at her eyes. She needed this. She couldn't run away from the truth now. The years fell away as she put her hand into Cyrus', much as she had when she was five years old, when she believed her shattered world had finally righted itself and she'd found another Daddy.

Chapter 20

As soon as they settled with their cups of tea into the cozy breakfast nook in the kitchen, Cyrus began the conversation on a lighter note.

"So are you married, Callie? Or is there an important man in your life?"

"Oh, no. I'm not married. There is a special someone and, you won't believe the irony of this, he's a doctor, a burn specialist."

"Huh! Is that how you met him? I wouldn't have dreamed of courting one of my patients, but the doctor-patient divide isn't as large as it used to be."

"No, actually, I spent some time in Belize and I met him there."

"Well, then that is definitely ironic. What's his name? Maybe I've heard of him."

"Probably not. He practices in San Francisco and he studied in Portland, Oregon at *Oregon Health Sciences University*. His name is Jake Lamb."

"Lamb, huh? That's interesting."

"What's interesting? Do you know him?"

"Oh, no. It's only, well, I've heard the name 'Lamb' just one other time. It doesn't matter, really," Cyrus changed the subject. "So you've been in San Francisco, then?"

"Yes. One of my lawyers—she was just an intern at the time, Leah—I'm staying with her. She was the tiny one with the auburn hair."

"I remember her. She passed loads of notes to the lawyers during the trial. I remember thinking she looked way too young to be an attorney."

"She still looks that way, only she's not an attorney any more. She's a doctor, too, in sports medicine."

"Well, good for her. It sounds like you are happy in San Francisco."

"The best part is my job. I'm putting together marketing displays for four different bookstores owned by the same man, V.J. Banks. He's the one who talked me into coming to see you."

"In that case, I owe him a debt of gratitude. We need to talk about what happened, Callie."

"I didn't want to come here until I heard about Constance's death. On the one hand, I knew she hated me for suing you both and exposing the truth. I could see it in her eyes. On the other, believe it or not, I was worried about you. How are you managing?"

Cyrus shifted uncomfortably, grief surfacing as he tried to find words to explain the loss of a loved one. "You know, I met Constance when we were both seventeen. We had the most basic of attachments, really. I loved her when she was just a girl and she loved me the same. Even when we'd graduated from our respective graduate programs and I got my M.D. and she started practicing outpatient therapy, we were still like teenagers together.

"Our shield cracked a little, though, when we weren't able to have children. I had found out I was completely sterile just before I met you. It was apparently from a bout with measles that I had as a child. I was morose, feeling quite inadequate, when I was given responsibility for the psychiatric care of a petite little girl who'd lost her entire family and been burned badly herself in a house fire."

Callie sat riveted and listened to her adoptive

father's story for the first time. Her memory of meeting Dr. Justice was muddled by the pain and grief she'd been mired in.

Cyrus continued. "You had bandages everywhere, but the first thing I noticed about you, Callie, were your remarkable eyes. They were golden-green like a panther, and you examined me just as intently as the cat would have. When we started to talk, though, your reserve, your suspicion melted away and you became the vulnerable little girl that you were. You broke my heart. You made me want to help you, to protect you and give you a home, because you didn't have one. No aunts, no uncles, no grandparents to take you home.

"I know I was wrong, now, to have asked Constance to take you in. She wasn't really the mothering type. As hard as we had tried to have our own children, I'm not sure I believe that she would have nurtured them effectively. She resented my time with you. She refused to feel the same empathy as I did and she didn't have it in her heart to open herself to your grief. It became easier for her to force you to deny your past, and ultimately, to put you out of our lives completely, by isolating you."

"Was she really that cruel, Cyrus? And how could you let her be?" Callie didn't understand what could make her mother so cold.

"What she did was cruel, but I still loved her. She never received any love or understanding from her own parents. She was raised by nannies, her basic needs met, but her soul never fed. I was the one who changed all of that for her. We were real and true soul mates.

"I never was good at standing up to her. Even after we lost everything and we moved around and finally landed here, she still browbeat me into thinking we could do better. I took a job landscaping for a local company and she took a reception job with Dr. Koepke.

"She seduced Dr. Koepke and then talked him into writing prescriptions for drugs that she could fill under different names and resell them at higher prices to drug-dependent housewives she would meet at the clinic. She claimed they were doing the women a favor by taking care of their pressing needs and it was all under the radar, so that it wouldn't look like he was widely prescribing certain, addictive medications.

"All was well, and I knew some of what was going on, because I had found several bottles of the medications in Constance's purse. She had told me about the sham, but not the affair. When one of the women died of an overdose and her husband found out in her journal that she'd been buying drugs from Constance, through Dr. Koepke's office, the proverbial crap hit the fan."

Callie smiled. Dr. Cyrus Justice had never to her knowledge cursed in her presence, and she found it endearing that he still refused to do so.

Cyrus smiled back sheepishly. He shrugged and kept going with his story. "Constance refused to be in trouble again and threatened to expose Dr. Koepke as the culprit for the affair and for the money-making scheme. He didn't, apparently, have the patience with her that I've always had. He went ballistic, pulling a 9mm from his desk drawer and confronting her in front of a whole waiting room full of patients. He shot her, point blank, and then apologizing to women and children alike who witnessed this devastation, he turned the gun on himself and shot himself in the head."

Callie winced. Trauma like that would never be erased from those people's minds.

Cyrus' sadness at the wrongful turn of events was apparent, but she could tell he was also basically frustrated by the woman's behavior. He'd been as much a victim of Constance Justice as she was. The people in the waiting room were her victims too. Callie was far too tired to hate her adoptive mother, but she vowed at that moment that she would never lose any more sleep wondering why Constance couldn't love her. Constance had only loved herself, and maybe Cyrus—she had probably loved him too.

Cyrus sat silently then and sipped his tea, the telling of the tale having exhausted him beyond reason. Callie let the peace continue as she companionably ate her snack.

They finished and Cyrus wiped his hands on a napkin and offered one to Callie.

"I am sorry for what we did to you, you know?"

Callie, usually guarded, finally allowed all of the hurt to surface so that she could let it go. "I know," she replied as a fat tear slid from her eye into her empty teacup.

"I've been mournful enough lately to recognize it in someone else's face. Why are you still so sad, Callie?"

It was time to let it out. The basic question—the question that was keeping her from loving Jake like he deserved—still needed an answer.

"Why couldn't you just love me, Daddy?"

Cyrus' heart broke wide open and tears burst into his shattered eyes. "I did love you, Callie. I still do. I was selfish, easily coerced, greedy, you name it. I'm far from perfect and I made huge mistakes, but I loved you from the moment you placed your hand in mine and I've missed you terribly, despite everything."

And with that, Callie broke down completely and fell into her father's arms, the only father she had, and grieved for the years they had lost, adversaries in a battle that neither one of them had ever wanted to fight.

Chapter 21

*C*yrus invited Callie to stay in his spare bedroom, but she found the tiny house obtrusive, little things reminding her of Constance Justice, and she decided that she would be more comfortable in a hotel.

As it turned out, Cyrus had done the landscaping for a bed and breakfast in Issaquah, just a short drive to the East. He called in a favor and they were happy to accommodate Callie while she was in town. She had no idea how long she would stay, but V.J. had offered her at least two weeks off. Now that she and Cyrus had put their cards on the table, she wanted to spend some more time with him.

Callie hadn't made a lot of friends during her time in the group home, but there were a few in Seattle that she still wanted to look up. Plus, there was a nurse at the hospital that had been particularly kind to Callie during her many treatments and Callie wanted to take her some flowers. All in all, it was enough to keep her around for a few more days, anyway.

When she'd been going through litigation with the Justices, her legal team had been *pro bono* from an organization called *Seattle Youth Alliance*, or *SeaYA*, for short. It was her third day in the Seattle area when she decided to pay them a visit. Leah had sent her good wishes and had asked Callie to say 'hi' to Avery Moss, the CEO, for her.

Though Leah had been adopted, she'd found out

just before leaving Seattle that her mother, the homeless teenager who'd left her behind, was Avery Moss' sister. This made Avery her uncle, not surprising since she'd felt a special connection to him while interning at *SeaYA*. Leah had exchanged a few letters with Avery over the years. She knew that he would get a high out of seeing Callie in person.

Callie had been one of the most unfortunate youths they'd had a chance to help at *SeaYA* and they still touted her case often to the government and public when they tried to get funds to further their aid to young people. Callie had no trouble getting face time scheduled with Avery Moss.

She walked into the downtown building and found it teeming with the same funky, youthful energy it had always had. Young people were hanging out in the lobby, playing pool and pinball, and making connections. A girl with spiky blond hair and tortoiseshell glasses met her warmly at reception and called a volunteer to lead her to the top floor offices of the *SeaYA* administration.

Avery Moss met Callie beside his secretary's desk and invited her into his spacious corner office. He was breathtakingly handsome with dark, curly, only slightly gray hair and sparkling blue eyes. He had the boyish good looks of a Kennedy, though his history with the company put him in his fifties. For years, he had been the most eligible bachelor in Seattle, until two years ago when he'd been snagged by a spritely, independent pottery sculptor who owned her own shop in Pioneer Square. Her given name was Americus Spaulding and she was the light of Avery's life. He called her Meri. He had photos of her and of their brand new baby boy displayed on the matching shelf to the right of his walnut desk.

When Callie stopped to admire the photos, she noticed another of a woman who looked very much like

Leah, but with light blond hair. She was pictured with a large, lumberjack-looking fellow and a little cherub of a boy, about three, judging by his size.

Avery noticed her perusal of the photos.

"You've seen my collection, then, haven't you, Callie? This is my wife, Meri, and my gorgeous son, Ian. This other photo," he said, gesturing, "is my sister, Sunny, with my Chief Financial Officer, Dennis Fulton. That's their bundle of joy, and my nephew, Syd. Cute, isn't he? Busy too. He was an unexpected joy, coming later in their lives, much like Ian did with us. I can't wait until Ian can keep up with him."

Avery was obviously very proud of his family as he beamed toward the familiar faces.

"So, Callie, you look wonderful. I hardly recognize the scrawny teenager we first saw here."

"I don't remember her very well either. I desperately needed help then and I'm so grateful that you gave it to me."

"That's what *Seattle Youth Alliance* is for. For the longest time, it was my only baby. I feel that cases like yours helped us cut our teeth. We are so much more adequate having had the experience.

"Have you been okay? You've left Seattle, haven't you?"

"I did. I live in San Francisco now, with Leah Westfield. She says 'hi,' by the way."

"Oh, how nice. How is Leah? I was sad to hear that such a great legal mind was defecting to the world of medicine."

"It makes her happy. Once she left law, she never really looked back."

"Good for her. She would be well suited for anything dealing with people. You remember that, don't you, that she could engage just about anyone?"

"Including me," she laughed. "I was about as

mistrustful and antisocial as a feral cat! I'd been isolated for so long, that it took me a while to trust anyone. Leah really brought me out of my funk. I'm still grateful for her friendship."

"So, why are you in town?" Avery sat back against his leather chair, letting Callie carry the conversation forward.

"You probably are aware, from the news, that Constance Justice was killed."

"That would have been hard to miss. It was unfortunately covered brutally by the press. Did you keep in touch with them, then?"

"No, I didn't, actually. I just felt sorry for Cyrus and I felt like I needed to come and get some answers and give my condolences."

"You know, I read through your background file last night just to refresh my memory about your case. I didn't figure you would stay in touch with the Justices. They'd been pretty horrible to you."

"They were and Cyrus is really still struggling with the guilt from that. I think we're going to work through it. After all, he is the only father I've got." Callie looked encouraged.

"That's wonderful to hear. I did a bit of reading about your birth family too. Our research department compiled quite a bit of data on them."

Callie hadn't anticipated that bit of news. She held her breath for a moment. She knew what had happened to her family, but she didn't really know how it happened. Because she had been so young when they were all killed, she didn't know anything about their backgrounds either. She found herself suddenly wondering if there was healing power in that piece of her past as well.

She barely dared to ask. "Do you think I could read through what they found?"

"Don't you already know what happened to them? I assumed you knew everything there was to know," Avery was perplexed. Surely her adoptive parents hadn't hidden her past completely. After all, she'd been five years old—old enough to remember what had happened.

"The Justices were never comfortable with any kind of discussion of my past. I know I nearly died in a house fire. I remember every awful, surreal detail of that night. I remember my brother and my sister curled up with me on my window seat with smoke surrounding us and stealing our every breath and I remember the horrible pain of the frigid night air on my burned skin. And I remember hearing the firefighters and paramedics saying 'she's the only survivor, the only one.'

"I remember my father being a perfect gentleman and my mother being strict, but fun-loving. We laughed a lot, my brothers and I, and they had started to include me in their games because I was finally getting old enough to understand.

"I remember feeling loved, absolutely and unconditionally, and I haven't felt that since," Callie finished, looking at Avery frankly.

Avery imagined every raw piece of the grief this girl had gone through. She didn't know everything, obviously. He figured, after what she had been through, that she might as well know.

"So you know nothing about the arson?"

"Arson?" Callie was at once alarmed and confused.

"Your parents' house didn't burn down accidentally. It was torched. They never caught the guy who did it, though it could have been any one of three men who'd burned down similar structures during a ten year span in Eastern Washington.

"Have you been back to your hometown?"

Callie was still trying to absorb the shock that her family had been killed intentionally. Five other members of her family had been murdered. It hadn't been a bad electrical wire or the old wood stove, as she'd always suspected because it was an old house. Somebody had deliberately set fire to the home.

Avery could see that Callie was deep in thought and hadn't heard his question. He rounded the desk and placed a hand on her shoulder.

"Are you going to be okay?"

Callie looked up, pulled out of her reverie, and blinked at Avery.

"I'm sorry, what did you ask me?"

"I wanted to know if you're going to be okay."

Callie wasn't sure, but she'd been through so much more. What she needed was information.

"Can I please look through the information you have?"

"You're welcome to it. Our research archives are one floor down. I'll call Sandy, my secretary, to help you find what you need."

Callie gathered her composure about her like an invisible cloak. Avery really did have to admire her spunk. She shook his hand and said, "Thank you for being so kind. You've helped me again and I appreciate it. If you'll have Sandy give me the information, I'd really like to make a cash contribution to *SeaYA* while I'm here. Your services are invaluable to the kids from this city. I wish there were more places like it in other cities. It would solve a lot of problems if children had someone reliable to turn to when a crisis developed at home or school. You provide that."

Avery was proud of *SeaYA*. They had helped their community a great deal and this young woman was living proof of the good they were doing.

Callie followed Sandy down the path to her past, hoping she could unravel any remaining mystery, and avenge the family she so fondly remembered.

Chapter 22

Callie spent four hours poring over the information *SeaYA*'s researchers had found. She felt like a witness to a gruesome murder—too engrossed to tear her eyes away, but desperately wanting to do so. The sheer speed with which her home had burned to the ground had tipped the fire inspector off that an accelerant must have been used. They never had a chance of getting out, especially Jamie and her parents, who had been downstairs and closer to the source of ignition.

Callie was extraordinarily lucky to have survived. The house was entirely engulfed by the time the first fire truck arrived. One brave and desperate volunteer firefighter had maneuvered a ladder truck to their bedroom window in hopes of finding someone alive. Neighbors gathered close by, telling the firefighters what they already feared—that there was a family in this house and none of them made it outside.

Callie relived her own emotions from that night, knowing how desperately she had wanted to save her brother and sister as they waited on the window seat with her. Her inadequacy still dug its ugly claws into her skull, making her head ache and the bile rise in her throat. Up until now, she had always felt like she failed them. This is why she suddenly welcomed the rage that overtook her as she read about the investigations into possible culprits. None of the three suspects, who had all been jailed within three years of the fire for other arson crimes, had admitted to or been linked to her family's fire.

Jeff Oakes, Stanley Crockett, and Wesley Shepherd—all were names that she would stamp onto her memory. Before she breathed her last breath, she would assure herself that none of these men actually killed her family. Somebody would pay, that she knew for sure.

Callie had made dinner plans with Cyrus, but she begged off, knowing that if she stayed at *SeaYA* until their six o'clock closing time, she would never make it back to Bellevue in time to meet Cyrus at the *Red Robin* there. She called him from her cell phone and made breakfast plans instead. When he found out what she was doing, he tried to talk her out of delving into that painful part of her past, but she stood firm.

Callie finished her research. The night janitor shut off lights and the door was locked behind her. She grabbed a Portobello burger at a Pioneer Square café. It was nearly nine o'clock by the time she drove back out to Issaquah. She was exhausted, far too tired to call Jake, who she knew would be worried about her by now.

Callie picked up a travel magazine on her way through the foyer and read it in bed after a long, hot shower. Her eyes slid closed and the periodical slipped softly to the floor as her dreams shut out the traumatic day and carried her away to balmier climes and warm, loving arms.

*C*allie awoke the next morning to a knock at her door. She startled awake and looked at the clock. It was already eight o'clock and she had to be up to meet Cyrus in Bellevue by ten. Still, she could afford to sleep in. She wondered who might be knocking at that hour, thinking it odd that the managers might rouse somebody this soon.

She opened the door to a lovely and fearsome sight. It was Jake in all of his magnificent glory, with stress emanating from his very core. He had obviously been wound up trying to track her down, but now with his success, his first act was to take the sleep-addled Callie into his arms and hold her like he would never let her go.

Callie, still in shock from seeing Jake at her door, in Washington State, at a remote Issaquah bed and breakfast, no less, responded silently, incredibly happy to have Jake holding her again, but entirely confused as to how he found her. Maybe she was still dreaming. All those warm muscles sure felt real, though.

Jake finally held her away from him for a moment and placed a tender kiss on her mouth.

"Don't you ever run away from me again, Callie of the White Sand. I can't take a third time."

"I didn't run away from you this time, Jake. I had some things I needed to take care of. I didn't see the need to involve you," Callie explained patiently.

"Don't you see that I am involved, Callie? I care about you. Therefore I worry about you. I had to talk Dr. I-Don't-Want-Another-Shift into taking two of mine for me so that I could track you down. I wouldn't have bothered, but then Leah told me where you were and I knew I needed to be here for you."

"I'm okay, Jake. Really. My father, Cyrus, and I have come to an understanding."

"How could you when he and his wife blatantly furthered your suffering?"

"Constance was the real culprit and she's gone now. Cyrus is desperately sorry for all I've been through."

"Yes, I realize that. He told me. He also told me that you spent a good portion of yesterday looking into the deaths of your birth family." Jake watched Callie's eyes as she absorbed this information.

"You've talked to Cyrus? When?" Callie marveled at his resourcefulness. Thank goodness she didn't need to hide from him!

"I got there about 6:30 this morning. He was a little bleary-eyed, but keen to know more about the man who is dating his daughter. He said you told him about me." Jake smiled charmingly, confident now that he knew his Callie was okay.

Callie couldn't help but smile back. She'd lamented more than once that this romantic little bed and breakfast would have been entirely more fun with Jake along. Now he was here.

"Jake Lamb, you amaze me. I thought you were a doctor, not a detective."

"Well I did get a little help from Leah, but only after extreme coercion. She was going to hold tight to what she knew, seeings how you didn't inform me yourself, but I convinced her that the gentle giant she's been friends with for so long only had your best intentions at heart." Jake kissed her more deeply this time, for emphasis.

"You look so sexy all rumpled up first thing in the morning," Jake observed, holding Callie away from him to admire her tousled black mane and drowsy eyes.

"Even in my floppy flannel PJ's?" Callie held her arms away from her and turned in a circle as if to show off all sides of her comfy get-up.

"Oh yes. Those I like, because I know exactly how many buttons will have to be undone to get inside them."

"You are naughty," Callie laughed. "What did you do with Bob while you were solving the mystery?"

"You won't believe this, but it turns out that Sean O'Carroll, Dr. Perfection himself, is a bonafide dog lover. He has a Newfoundland and a Burmese Mountain Dog, both lovely ladies just the right size and temperament to keep Bob company. You should have seen Bob roll his eyes at me when I asked him if he'd be okay there. Bob is just fine. I don't know if I'll be able to talk him into coming home again."

"You know, I don't know Sean very well yet, but I have a feeling I'm going to like him," Callie offered.

"One thing's for sure. Leah likes him. A lot."

"It's great to see her happy," Callie said, genuinely relieved that Leah was doing so well in the wake of what had happened to her.

"So you've been traveling all night?" She asked Jake as she observed for the first time the shadows lurking about his bright blue eyes.

"I took the red eye so that I could get here as soon as possible. I only have three days until I have to get back."

"Maybe I'll fly back with you if I can get some things settled here," Callie contemplated, knowing she would soon have to tell Jake everything. He deserved to know all of her past, now that she was finally coming to realize it. She could no longer deny that the baggage made her who she was today.

"In the meantime, I have a whole two hours until I have to meet my father for breakfast. Maybe you would like to get some sleep in the meantime," she suggested.

"Sleep? Who wants to sleep? You are far too delicious in the morning. There is no way, if you take me to that bed, that I'm going to sleep," Jake teased.

"Well then, what are we waiting for?" Callie smiled suggestively at this man that she loved and gave herself over to the abandon that she knew only with him.

Afterward, both of them were reluctant to leave their warm embrace and the confines of the queen-sized four-poster bed. Callie knew, though, that she needed to get in the shower if she had any hope of being on time for breakfast.

She chatted with Jake while she got ready. He planned to stay in while she went out to breakfast and catch up on some sleep. His love hormones were kicking in and pulling his eyes shut. But he wanted to talk with Callie until she left.

"I think your father is really a good guy at heart," he offered. "I just think he made mistakes that he really regrets. He lost an awful lot by being so foolish: his money, his medical license, his home, not to mention his only child. It's nice to see him trying to make up for some of it."

"Cyrus does mean well. He's desperately lonely without Constance. As much as she browbeat him, he loved her more than anything," Callie replied.

"He asked me something sort of odd before he told me where I could find you."

"What was that?"

"He was fascinated with my last name, Lamb, and he wanted to know where I grew up."

Callie turned from the mirror where she'd been applying her mascara.

"That is weird. Funny that you should bring that up, because you and I have never really talked about where you grew up either," Callie said.

"I don't know, Callie. It seems to me like neither of us has delved much into our pasts because yours was obviously so pain-riddled and complicated that I didn't want to pry. And my past, well, it has nothing to do with the way I am now."

"The past is always relevant to how we are now. If there is something I've learned in the past two days, it's that," Callie insisted. "Where did you grow up, Jake? I want to know just because it's interesting, because I want to know everything about you."

"We moved around a little, my Dad and I, but we

mostly stayed in or around Tonasket, Washington."

"You're from Washington State? I always assumed you were from Oregon because you went to school there." Callie was surprised that Jake hadn't mentioned it since she was from Washington also.

"I am. That's why neither of us talks funny," he offered light heartedly.

"You know, Tonasket isn't very far from where I originally lived. My family's house was in Republic."

Jake's mouth ran dry as he realized what Callie had just said.

"I thought you were raised in Western Washington."

"I was raised here, but my birth family lived in the Northeastern part of the State. I ended up in Seattle when I was flown here to *Seaview Medical Center* for treatment of my burns."

Jake seemed upset, which made no sense to Callie. She hadn't misled him about where she was originally from. He had just never asked.

He withdrew from the conversation suddenly, admitting his utter exhaustion, and suggesting that he might be allowed to sleep while Callie finished getting ready.

Callie kissed Jake on the forehead and he rolled over to face away from the door. She slipped her loafers on quietly and slipped out to call a cab, careful not to disturb her tired lover.

Jake wasn't asleep as the door clicked quietly shut. He was suddenly wide awake because he knew his luck had just run out.

Chapter 23

*W*ith a flimsy excuse note pardoning his absence, Jake left the bed and breakfast at noon in his rental car and headed North on I-405, through the bustling Eastern suburbs of Seattle and on to a calmer stretch of freeway. He arrived in the town of Monroe, surprised to see that modernization had hit the cattle town. There was actually more than just a prison there now as new stores and restaurants lined Highway 2, which ran East from Seattle to Leavenworth, Washington.

Jake took the side street he knew would lead him to the imposing gothic walls of the State Reformatory. Jake took care to remove his gold college ring and to change from his penny loafers to athletic slip-ons with no metal on them. He was ready to go through security.

All during the drive, Jake had convinced himself that Callie was a lost cause. She would never forgive him for who he was to her. Heartbroken as he was with this knowledge, he wanted desperately to do just this one thing for her.

As he passed through one security door and then another and into a holding room where he could meet his father face to face, Jake weighed what he would say to the man who had raised him until he was put in prison when Jake was fifteen years old. Jake's mom, Greta Lamb, had left them when he was a baby. Wesley Shepherd was the only parent Jake had ever known.

He walked in cuffed at the wrists and ankles and

Jake noted that his father, once as large in stature as Jake, had shrunk and stooped with age. Wes' hair was completely gray and his skin hung slack around vivid blue eyes. Jake imagined this was what he himself would look like when he was in his sixties. At least he wouldn't be aging in prison, as his father was destined to do.

Jake had called ahead to the prison to let them know he was coming, so Wes was prepared for the visit. He'd already put on the impenetrable mask that was his trademark with his fellow prisoners and his son. Wes Shepherd was known as a cold S.O.B., without a conscience, and he regarded his son warily now, wondering what could have compelled him to come here.

"So I see the all-important doctor has come to bestow his presence on his poor, innocent father. What's the occasion? Are you dying?"

"Nice sarcasm, Dad. You and I both know you're far from innocent."

"Not that any of these people will listen, but I'm just as innocent as I say I am, of some of the things I'm accused of, anyway."

"Cut the crap, Dad. You took me with you."

"I was a single dad. I couldn't just leave my five-year-old son home alone when I went out at night."

"But you took me when I was twelve too. I think you wanted to teach me your craft, sick as it was."

"It beat going to bars. Women would fling themselves at me in bars. Your mother had been a no-good floozy who dumped you and me as soon as she could find a ride out of town. I didn't need any more women screwing us up, so I had other hobbies."

"You torched things, Dad, and that got you off. I watched you light everything from gasoline to dynamite to hydrogen. Then you and I would return to town and follow the emergency vehicles to the fire to watch them put it out. I remember you would 'wake' me up to show me the fire."

"It was fun too. I figure I must have burned down at least fifty structures, don't you think?"

"I wasn't counting, Dad. I do know this, though: Somebody died and that's how you ended up here."

"There wasn't supposed to be anybody in that old church," Wes defended. "I never imagined that the Deacon's wife would have kicked him out to the doghouse for the night and that the doghouse would be the church."

Jake felt the familiar wave of nausea he experienced so often when he knew what atrocities his father had committed while Jake pretended to be asleep in the truck.

"That deacon is the reason you are here, but I have to know about another place. I'm not sure if you burned it down, but I recall when I was about twelve that you lit a propane torch and tossed it in the window of an old Victorian-style house and I don't recall just exactly where it was."

"Oh, there were a couple of Victorians; Just crappy old houses that needed a lot of work. One of them was just this side of Goldendale. We had gone down to visit my sister and I wanted to see how their fire department operated.

"The other one was really cool because it had a wrap-around porch with old-fashioned carved spindles in the railing. It looked gorgeous all lit up, framed in fire, as it was. It was on the edge of town in Republic, just over Wauconda pass from where we were living in Tonasket at the time."

Jake's throat constricted as he held back his anger. Just as he suspected, Wes had admitted only to a fraction of the buildings he burned down, and he certainly would never have acknowledged to authorities that he was responsible for burning anything down. He always claimed bragging rights with his son.

Jake wiped his face with both of his hands to erase the horror from it and sat there with his face covered for a moment. He took a deep breath.

"Are you aware that an entire family perished in that fire?" He eyed his father coldly, assessing him to see if he would tell the truth.

"One of them survived. I read about it and the State police came to talk to me about it after I was put away in here. They pulled somebody out." Wes had the good grace to look ashamed. This took Jake by surprise. His father had never shown any amount of remorse before.

"How do you think that little girl felt losing her whole family and getting burned from head to toe in the process?"

Wes hung his head briefly and spoke softly. Jake was mesmerized.

"I never torched a place with the intention of anyone getting hurt. I swear I didn't see any cars around the place or any lights on downstairs that would have tipped me off to people living there."

"It was the middle of the night," Jake shot back, his reverie broken. "The cars were probably in the garage out back or somewhere outside the house, since it was an old house."

"The fact is, Son, that I didn't know because they were in a whole different town. I picked that house out randomly and I made a stupid mistake."

"A mistake? Is that what you call it? You make me sick. I can't believe you're my father. You're a monster." Jake suddenly knew what it was like to swim in the deep end of the ocean.

"You heard from your sister that I'm a doctor, didn't you?" Jake spat.

Wes nodded in reply, his eyes sad as he watched his

only son rage from the depths of his disappointment.

"Did she tell you what kind of doctor I am?" His father shook his head. "I'm a burn specialist, Dad. When you went to prison for burning somebody to death, I went to live with my aunt and then I got out of Dodge as soon as I was old enough. I changed my last name to my mom's. I took my scarred psyche and I buried it as deep as it would go. Then I smiled and charmed and studied my way into as many scholarships as I could get and went to college and then to medical school.

"I just knew that if I started to help people that maybe I could erase some of the damage that you had done. I also needed to repent for never stopping you. I had that power, Dad. I could have turned you in at some point, but out of some demented sense of loyalty to my only parent, I never did.

"I love what I do—fixing people who are in pain, scarred for life. Every person I help repays heaven for what you did.

"Do you even know how many people you killed? I bet you know exactly how many because that's how your sick mind works."

His father spoke softly, resigned, acknowledging his son's ire, but refusing to join it.

"Why did you come here, Son?"

"Because I had to know about that one fire, the Victorian," Jake replied, his chest still heaving with emotion.

"Why did you want to know about that one?"

"It meant everything, Dad. You see, I know that survivor and I love her and I've finally realized that no matter how many people I fix, I cannot undo the harm that you've done. She's lost to me as much as you are because she'll never forgive me for being the son of the man who killed her family."

"For what it's worth, Jake, I do have regrets," his

father began to apologize, for the first time, to his son.

"Don't, Dad. You've always been frigid, collected, calculating. That's how you are. That's how you'll always be to me. Don't start getting all apologetic, because I don't buy it. Your parole board might, God forbid. I hope you spend the rest of your miserable life in here, sorry or not. You're not my father, so quit calling me 'Son,' Wes. I hate you for what you've done to Callie, to me, and to yourself."

With that, tears stinging his eyes, Jake stood and turned his back on the man who had raised him and walked to the security door to wait for the guard to let him out. Wesley Shepherd just sat there and watched his son retreat, knowing there was nothing he could do or say to bring him back.

Chapter 24

Callie's breakfast with Cyrus was delicious. He chose a restaurant with a daily breakfast buffet and they both gorged themselves on strawberry waffles, carrot cake muffins, scrambled eggs with sausage gravy, and fresh pineapple. Callie hadn't stuffed herself like that in ages and when Cyrus offered to take her shopping at Bellevue Square, she welcomed the opportunity to walk off some of the calories. Besides, she knew that Jake could use the extra sleep should she stay away a little longer.

She and Cyrus shopped companionably in the mall teeming with Christmas décor and harried holiday shoppers. She refused to let him buy anything for her. She didn't feel comfortable with that kind of familiarity yet and she had more money to spend than he did. She bought some kidskin leather boots and a couple of wool pencil skirts that were on sale. They would work well with her career wardrobe.

She had always pictured Jake as a flannel shirt sort of guy too and they were hard to come by in California, so she picked up a couple of extra-large, tall flannels for him. She also happened by a gift shop that had writing pens with purebred dogs atop them. She found one with a bloodhound on it that was a ringer for Bob and she bought it for Jake. He would love it and he could keep it in the upper pocket of his lab coat. It was sure to get kids' attention.

She picked up intricate, hand-blown, glass ornaments to put in her carry-on for Leah and V.J..

It was about two o'clock when she and Cyrus sat down with lattes and contemplated their purchases. Cyrus shifted on the metal bench so that he could face Callie.

"I can see in your face how taken you are with this Jake fellow. I take it you're glad I told him where he could find you."

"I was shocked to see him, but yeah, I guess it was okay. I just didn't want him involved in my whole family mess."

"We're not so messy," Cyrus offered gently. "I think things will work out okay, with baby steps."

"Sure they will, Dad, but I didn't know that when I left San Francisco."

"That's true," Cyrus replied. "You know, I quizzed Jake on where he was from and he gave me an interesting answer."

"He mentioned that. You seemed familiar with the 'Lamb' name when I brought it up a few days ago too. Why is it important?" Callie sipped at her hazelnut latte and waited for her father's answer.

"I once met a woman named Greta Lamb at *Seaview Medical Center*, the same place I first met you."

"Isn't 'Lamb' a fairly common name?" Callie asked.

"I'm not sure, but the reason I remember this woman is because she asked about you. She didn't know your name, but she wanted to know about the little girl from Republic that she'd read about in the paper. She wanted to know how you were doing and she had looked me up at the hospital for that very purpose. It was about three months after we had taken you home. I was afraid to share too much with Greta, to compromise our privacy, but I assured her you had found a new family and that you were well."

"Did you ask her why she wanted to know about me?"

"I did. She said she had an idea who had hurt you and killed your family. She said she felt somewhat responsible for this man's actions. I think she was looking for vindication. If you were okay, then she could feel less guilty."

"Did you know we were the victims of arson?" Callie tried to piece it all together.

"Up to that point, I hadn't really tried to find out. I didn't think it mattered how you had come to us. I figured it would hurt you more to have to delve into the past, so Constance and I always discouraged talk of your family and of the fire.

"It didn't keep me from doing research about the fire, though. I contacted the fire marshall and the newspapers from the area and got all of the information I could about your house fire. I subscribed to two of the papers and kept tabs on the news from your hometown. It was several years before any suspects were named and this was all after they had been indicted on other charges."

"I know the names: Jeff Oakes, Stanley Crockett, and Wesley Shepherd," Callie listed them methodically.

"You've been doing some of your own research," Cyrus commented. "Two of these men were small-time arsonists, burning outbuildings and abandoned shacks and operating mostly in the Inland Empire area and one in the Tri-Cities area. None of them admitted to the crime. One, though, Callie, had lived very nearby, as close as Tonasket, which is only an hour's drive from your hometown."

"Who was it?" Callie sought the answers, even if only to satisfy her own curiosity.

"It was Wesley Shepherd. I did a background check on him and he was married once, to a woman named

Greta Lamb."

Callie marveled at the irony, and then the pieces clicked into place. Jake Lamb was from Tonasket. He'd said so. With trepidation she asked her father one final question, almost unwilling to know the answer.

"Did they have any children?" She asked in a tiny voice. Cyrus had to strain to hear her.

"Just one boy and Greta apparently divorced his father when their son was just a baby. His given name was Jacob Shepherd."

Callie's eyes brimmed with tears. It had to be more than coincidence. Were Jacob Shepherd and Jake Lamb one and the same? Jake had been so distant, almost angry when he had learned where she was from. Did he know? She wondered. Was Wesley Shepherd the man who had murdered her family? More importantly, was he Jake Lamb's father?

Cyrus' wise, chocolate eyes saw the heartbreak in his daughter's face.

"It is possible that there is a whole Lamb family in that area and that Jake has nothing to do with the fire or the man who set it," Cyrus suggested hopefully. He patted Callie's knee for emphasis.

She nodded, trying to keep the tears at bay. There must be a simple explanation. The fates could never be so cruel. Or could they?

*C*allie knew the answer the minute she walked through the door to her room at the bed and breakfast. Jake was up, and showered, his chestnut curls gelled into place. He was definitely not rested, though. The shadows only deepened around his cerulean eyes. He sat in the corner chair, absently reading her travel magazine, and watching the door. When Callie came in, he stood in greeting. Callie's heart fell into her shoes. Jake looked crestfallen.

Callie approached cautiously, every instinct screaming at her to walk back out the door. She set her bags down and offered one to Jake.

"I bought a few things for you," she spoke quietly, shattering the silence between them.

"You didn't have to do that," Jake reddened, accepting the gift. "I wondered what kept you so long."

"I figured that you needed to sleep, so I took Cyrus up on his offer to go shopping."

"Did you have fun?"

"Yes."

"Good. That's good," Jake licked his lips nervously and wiped his big hands on the legs of his chinos.

"Jake. Why don't you tell me what's bothering you?" Callie offered, knowing that she didn't want to hear the answer to her question.

"I don't know where to start," he admitted. "Can I just hold you for a minute?"

Callie stepped into his embrace and he let out a whoosh of air. They stood there for the longest time, rocking in a primal rhythm, neither wanting to air this thing that would break both of their hearts.

Callie spoke first. "It's okay, Jake. You can tell me anything."

"I know that. You've shared pretty much everything with me—your scars, the abuse you suffered as a child, and your fears about letting someone into your life. You let me in, Callie, and that is so precious to me, that you trusted me that much."

"Why do I sense that you think I'm going to regret that?"

"Because I can't be the man you share your life with. I'm only the beginning. You're going to move on and move past me and find the true love of your life. I'm just a bump in the road."

"Are you trying to break up with me? I don't understand. I thought we both felt the same," Callie drew away from Jake, not willing to let him hold her any longer.

"I love you, Callie, but I'm not the man for you. You've shared everything with me and I've pried a lot of it out of you, but I've never done the same. I've never admitted to my past.

So there it was.

"Are you going to tell me what it is about your past that means we can't be together?"

"That's only fair, don't you think?"

Callie nodded and waited expectantly.

Jake sighed again and sat down on the edge of the bed. Callie chose to remain standing.

"I'm the reason your real family is dead."

Callie blanched. She hadn't expected him to take this approach.

"How can that be? They died in a house fire."

"Tell me about them, Callie. I want to know just what and who you lost."

"I can't," she began and then saw Jake's eyes pleading with her. "Okay. My father was Barron Jones and he was kind, patient, and fun, never cross and he really doted on us girls. My little sister was Libby, short for Elizabeth and she could put the biggest twinkle in my dad's eyes you could ever see. She was three when she died. My oldest brother, Timothy, was nine and he was the planner in the family, not always responsible, but always in charge of us kids. My other brother, James, or Jamie, as we called him, was seven and he had asthma, but it didn't stop him from playing with us full-tilt. My mom, Cecilia Jones, was strict with us, but she had the biggest heart. Her smile, as my dad said, could light up the night sky. I remember lots of laughing, joking, hugging—warmth and security everywhere I turned. We were just that kind of family." Her voice was wistful. Her tone revealed that she knew just exactly what she had lost.

Callie finished her story, looking down at her hands. She looked up surprised to see the normally happy, light-hearted Jake dissolving into tears. She resisted the urge to comfort him, for he was feeling just a fraction of the pain she'd carried with her for nearly twenty years.

He met her solemn eyes. "My father lit that fire, Callie. I was in the truck waiting for him. I was nearly twelve years old and he'd been lighting up the night sky all over Eastern Washington since I was three or four. I never did a thing to stop him, even when I was old enough to know that what he was doing was wrong.

"I've spent nearly every moment since I was sixteen trying to make up for covering up for my dad, but my efforts have been inadequate, obviously because now I realize that my ignorance, my silence, cost the woman that I love her family."

Callie felt no sympathy and her anger flared. "How could you keep quiet about something that big, Jake? I understand that you were just a kid, but you are responsible."

"I know that, Callie, and I'm going to have to live with that everyday that you're not with me," Jake admitted.

"There is something weird about this, though." He continued.

"What's that?" She demanded.

"You don't seem surprised that it was my dad who lit the fire."

"Cyrus and I just had the most interesting conversation. I hoped what I suspected wasn't true, but after putting the pieces of the puzzle together and hearing your admission, it would be pretty difficult to feign surprise."

"Cyrus figured it out? How?"

"Apparently your mother checked in on me after she read the news of the fire. She claimed partial responsibility as well."

"I had no idea my mom kept tabs on me or my father."

"Obviously she did," Callie replied. "Cyrus only looked into the arson after she approached him. Hearing your last name triggered him to ask you about your origins. Frankly, I'm surprised you didn't lie to him."

"I've made mistakes, but I'm not a liar. You've had time to think about this, Callie. Surely you know me better than that."

"Hardly. I came in here with the intention of finding out if my assumption was truth. I had no idea that you were actually there when your father started the fire. Honestly, Jake, I don't know what to make of all of this. I'm tired, that's what I am," Callie admitted, resigned.

"I can't believe of all of the women in the world, that I found you. There must be a reason, Callie."

"Well then you need to see if you can figure out that reason," Callie's heart steeled. She had so little control over the events in her life. This was something about which she had a choice. If Jake's father would never pay for his crime, then some way, somehow, his son was going to find a way to pay. If losing her was payment, then so be it.

Jake watched her visibly slip through his fingers. His Callie was lost to him. There was nothing more to say. He nodded in acknowledgment and grabbed his travel bag and with shoulders slumped in defeat, he turned tail and bolted out the door.

Callie simply sat and stared forlornly at the shopping bag with his flannels and pen in it. She was full of love and hope when she bought them. How could the world go so topsy-turvy in just a few hours' time?

Chapter 25

Leah didn't know the details of Jake's time in Seattle with Callie. All she knew was that things had gone terribly wrong. The report from Sean O'Carroll was that Jake showed up at his house to get Bob two days earlier than Sean expected him. His eyes were red-rimmed and he said little other than 'thanks' for caring for his dog.

Jake went on his way with Bob the bloodhound and nobody heard from him for a week. He pawned off three of his shifts and, after much discussion among their lunch group, sans Leah, but with her blessing, all agreed to send Lanny over to Jake's to check on his well-being.

Lanny went to Jake's townhouse on a Friday evening after work. After much coaxing, Jake invited him in. The apartment was in shambles. The normally tidy Jake hadn't cleaned one dish or put one piece of laundry in the washer. The stench from Jake himself was almost more than Lanny could handle. It was, according to Lanny's report, the worst possible state their friend could have been in. Even Bob was in disgrace, unable to meet Lanny's gaze and the usually well-exercised dog seemed lethargic.

It took Lanny several hours and many uncomfortable silences to extract information from Jake. All he gleaned was that Callie had kicked Jake to the curb and that Jake accepted full responsibility for being booted.

Jake returned to work the following week, reluctantly, but because he felt guilty giving away any more of his shifts this close to Christmas.

Callie finally arrived home the same week. Leah was ready to kill her for keeping them all in suspense. Leah was still apartment-bound for two more weeks and then, after four weeks of physical therapy, she was going to be allowed to go back to work. She'd gone stark-raving mad hanging out within the confines of her apartment, especially without Callie to distract her. Her moms stayed long enough to make sure she could manage the navigation of the apartment without them, but they had gone back to Seattle a week ago. Sean was a welcome distraction, but she only got his company when he wasn't working which wasn't often.

When she heard the key in the lock and Callie opened the door and turned to grab her luggage, Leah pounced.

"Where have you been?" Leah screeched from her perch on the couch, sending Beulah streaking to the back bedroom.

Callie jumped visibly, then relaxed when she saw Leah's face. Welcome, worry, and boredom were etched into Leah's features. Callie felt a brief stab of guilt. She should have called. She finished bringing her suitcases into the living room and plopped herself on the couch next to Leah.

"I'm sorry, Leah. Have you been going totally crazy here?"

"Don't change the subject," Leah objected. "I asked where you've been. Nobody has heard from you for a week, including Cyrus. I called him. And Jake, well, that's a different subject entirely. This whole nomad thing that you did for years on your own, well it doesn't really work now that you have people here who care about you!" Leah scolded Callie.

"I know. Really, I am sorry. I had something I needed to do. I went to Eastern Washington, to Republic, where our house burned to the ground."

"Wow," Leah breathed. "How was that? Did you drive the snowy roads over there? I've done that before with my moms. It's real winter in Eastern Washington this time of the year."

"Actually, I took a plane to Spokane and rented a car from there. They haven't gotten a whole lot of snow yet, though I was sweating an oncoming storm quite a bit when I was getting ready to leave. As it turned out, it did snow, but not enough to make a mess of the roads.

"Eastern Washington is beautiful. There are more trees than I remember and breathtaking mountains further North. Republic is tiny, historical. It looks a little like an old-western style town and there are lakes and rivers nearby that are just gorgeous. I remember playing at Curlew Lake when I was a little kid, catching crawdads and fishing for bass. It looks just the same as it did then."

"Did you go to your old property?" Leah listened and observed her friend. Callie still had all of her ethereal sparkle, but she looked frazzled around the edges. Leah sensed a deep emotional exhaustion, which was understandable given Callie's activities of late.

"Isn't it funny? But I had no idea where to look for it. I know we were in town, but we had at least two city lots worth of land and a huge garage to one side of the house. I didn't think the garage burned down. Also I remembered an aging stand of poplars on the North side. That's why our neighbors never heard us yelling at our window the night of the fire.

"I ended up going to the town library to find news archives and find out where the fire was. The librarian knew who I was. I didn't even have to tell her. She said I was the spitting image of my mother. She did volunteer work with the library on a regular basis. The librarian cried when she talked about my family."

"That's understandable. I'll bet the whole town grieved your loss," Leah offered.

"I think they did. The librarian showed me the archives and then volunteered to caravan with me to the site of our house. The house had been a total loss and the people who bought the property kept the garage and tried to rebuild the new house on the footprint of the old. It had none of the same craftsmanship or character of the old house. Plus, our house was the yellow of early morning sunshine and in need of a paint job. The new house was hunter green with white trim. It did me good to be there, though. It was almost as if I could confirm that the whole thing happened by knowing that my house and my family were truly gone.

"My father's family homesteaded in Wauconda, this little one-horse town directly to the East of Republic and the original house still stood there. My dad was one of only two kids and his brother died as a teenager in a car accident, so when my grandparents were moved to an old-folks home, my dad sold the ranch. The new owners were kind enough to show me the house where my dad grew up."

"Sounds like the locals were really friendly to you," Leah commented.

"Oh, it was amazing. It's no wonder I was never happy in Seattle. I think the small-town portion of my upbringing stuck in my sub-conscience. You know, Ferry County is enormously economically depressed, but those people are in it together, neighbor helping neighbor. It was encouraging to know that people still live that way."

Moving on, Leah spoke again, gently, "I'm going to have to ask about Jake, Callie. He's my old friend too."

"Jake didn't share when he came back?" Callie was reluctant to tell the whole story.

"Jake is a bona fide mess. He's only told Lanny that you broke up with him and for good reason."

Callie was weary, but she'd missed Leah and she owed her the truth. "Have you got any coffee?" She asked, ready to settle in for a good talk.

"You bet. You can get us both a cup," Leah offered generously.

Even Leah was in tears by the time Callie finished her story. It was extraordinarily cruel that Jake and Callie had met not once, but twice, and fallen in love, only to find that their destinies were fatefully intertwined. She didn't blame Callie at all for being angry at the circumstances, but she did have to jump to the defense of Jake.

"He was only a kid, you know. How many of us stand up to our parents when we're only ten or eleven years old? I'm not sure I could have turned one of my moms in to the authorities, even if I'd known what she was doing was against the law. And think. That would have made him an orphan too."

"He ended up being an orphan anyway," Callie said.

"But he never had to wonder whether he did the right thing turning his father in. His dad made his own mistakes and he is paying for them. Now Jake is paying for them too."

"I still can't forget about it, Leah. He had the power to keep his father from torching my family's house. If he had stopped him that night, we wouldn't even be here now."

"And you wouldn't be the person you are either— intelligent, worldly, wise…"

"Scarred, suspicious, quiet…" Callie finished for her friend.

"You aren't, Callie. You're one of the strongest, bravest people I know and it is the direct result of being a survivor," Leah looked frankly into her friend's eyes.

Callie reached immediately for her friend, careful not to upset her cast and gave her a big hug.

"Thank you for saying that. I am strong and I'm getting stronger every day. In a way, Jake helped with that. But there is still part of me missing. My siblings were my soul mates and their loss left a gaping hole in me that will never heal. I still feel like Jake is partly responsible."

"That's understandable, Callie, but do me a favor."

"What?"

"I want you to remember how long it took to get the courage up to finally make the Justices accountable for their crimes against you. I want you to remember how disloyal it felt to do so. I want you to think about how you still feel about Cyrus, despite all of it."

"Okay, Leah. I get your point. I'll think about it."

"In the meantime," Leah pointed out, "You had better call V.J. and let him know you made it home safely. He's been worried about you too. I had to reassure him several times that he wasn't wrong to let you head to the wilds of Washington State. I swear that man needs to step a few feet outside of California sometime. I'm pretty sure he thinks that San Francisco is the only civilized place on Earth."

Callie laughed. That was V.J. all right—the quintessential San Franciscan. She hugged her friend carefully once more and retreated to her room with her bags to call V.J.

Chapter 26

*D*octor Sean O'Connell shocked everyone on Christmas Eve and scooped Leah from her couch and into his Lexus and took her to his parents' house in Malibu. Callie would never forget the way tiny Leah melted into Sean's arms. She beamed like a beacon on a storm-tossed sea. The pang of jealousy was fleeting because her friend had waited forever for this man. Callie was happy for her.

Callie and V.J. had a cozy Christmas dinner at an exclusive downtown restaurant, opting for a sushi opener and filet mignon over traditional turkey dinner. They made a champagne toast to the baby Jesus. V.J. gave Callie a dainty filigreed gold locket for Christmas. Callie opened it to find inside a picture of V.J. sticking out his tongue. She laughed until she cried.

She gave V.J. his hand-blown ornament and a leather-bound journal with his initials embossed in script across the front. V.J. had a creative mind, Callie had noticed, and she encouraged him to start journaling his thoughts and ideas as a form of therapy. V.J. was touched by the very personal gift.

After he drove her home, V.J. kissed Callie on her forehead and bid her goodnight. She went to bed on Christmas night, thankful for her good friend V.J., but missing Jake. She wondered what he was doing, if he was okay. She had no right to wonder, but, Lord help her, she did.

*J*ake got drunk. He already had a cab arranged to pick him up at midnight and cart him home. His aunt taught him the habit of going to Christmas mass. That was what he should have been doing, but he felt the need to drown out this Christmas. Mai-Tais and Long Island Iced Teas seemed the best way.

The bartender suddenly became his best friend and he told him tales of saving lives, bringing back to life patients who had no chance when they arrived at the doors of   *St. Katherine's*. When he was drunk enough, he switched to tales of arson and the taking of lives. The bartender listened intently and then let him wallow, which Jake was thankful for. It was easily the most miserable Christmas he could imagine. He missed Callie with an ache that responded to no amount of salve, or booze, in this case. He wondered how she was and hoped that she wasn't alone. He didn't know if she'd come back from Washington yet and he wished her well with a toast, wherever she was.

*B*y the next morning, Jake couldn't have been any sorrier for the way he'd spent his Christmas. His head pounded and his eyes were as dry as the Mohave. If the world made any sense, his mouth would still taste like the Long Island Iced Tea he'd polished off just before midnight. Instead it tasted like the smell of cat poop.

Jake moaned and rolled over in bed to find Bob staring at him, his need to take his first morning pee written in his eyes. Jake felt the same urge.

"I hear you, Buddy. Me first, though." Jake went to the bathroom to relieve himself. He winced as he returned and reached for his jeans and a sweatshirt. 'Should've taken another Ibuprofen before bed,' he thought.

He rinsed his mouth quickly with mouthwash and slipped bare feet into his loafers. He didn't feel like fumbling with tube socks on a morning like this. Rubbing his face to bring the circulation back to the surface, Jake stumbled out to the hallway, grabbed Bob's leash off the wall hook, and carefully navigated the two flights of stairs with Bob in tow. Bob said thank you to the nearest tree and Jake wished for the hundredth time that he could do the same without the neighbors complaining.

If only he could be a bloodhound. Bob had it made. He now had two girlfriends—Gracie & Casey, Sean's dogs, and he strutted about like God's gift to all female canines. Jake was pretty sure that Bob had his back too. He really was thankful for his best friend, especially now. He'd been pretty low the last couple of weeks. If he was a drinking man, he might just go find a pint and continue what he'd started last night. But he wasn't. Jake truly was more responsible than that. He was still a man worth admiring, he knew and he had a reputation and a career to uphold. No amount of self-deprecation could steal his accomplishments as a person and as a physician.

It would never be enough, though, to bring back the one thing he wanted most—a life with Callie. It was his fate to lose her, difficult as that was to accept. He was grappling with it and good sense was prevailing. He was just glad that Christmas was over, so he could get on with life. 'If the hangover would ever quit,' he thought ruefully.

Chapter 27

Exactly two weeks after Christmas Day, Jake received a letter in the mail from his aunt wishing him belated 'Happy Holidays' and informing him that his father had been released from prison. Apparently the parole board really had bought into good behavior and a remorseful attitude. His father had gotten thirty years for killing the deacon in the church fire, and he'd only served seventeen.

Jake could only imagine what the family of Deacon Rivers felt about Wesley Shepherd being let back into society. The man had paid minimally for all of the damage he'd done. But then the law really had no idea the extent of his crimes. Only Jake was privy to that information.

Jake had planned to leave Callie alone. There really was no reason for their lives to intersect any longer. He could avoid parties where Leah might invite the both of them and he could steer clear of the *V.J.'s* stores, where he knew she spent a good portion of her time. San Francisco was a big city—plenty of room for both of them.

When he found out about his father's parole, however, he felt compelled to look her up once again. It was Tuesday, so he knew she'd be at the *V.J.'s* on Haight. His shift didn't start until three, so he swung by just after lunch.

Callie thought she was seeing an apparition when

she looked up from her pile of books and posters and saw   Dr. Jake Lamb silhouetted in the sun from the display window. She shielded her eyes against the penetrating glow that surrounded him and he knelt down to where she was sitting on the floor, so she would no longer be blinded.

He came slowly and deliciously into focus.

"Hi Jake," was her ineffectual greeting, and Callie kicked herself as her rebellious insides did a jig.

"Hi Callie." Jake was just as taken, drinking her in, her hair like black silk cascading down her shoulders, her skin like fresh cream. There were shadows in her green eyes, fatigue in the set of her shoulders. He silently hoped that he wasn't the one responsible for those. Then he remembered how miserable he'd been himself and felt a smidgen of hope that she might be feeling the same.

They sat there like that for a few minutes, examining each other, looking deeper, speaking without talking, but all that came out were questions. Callie finally moved to sit at one of the nearby reading tables and Jake followed suit.

"Jake, why are you here?"

"I found out today that my father has been paroled from prison."

"I wasn't aware that he was still in prison," Callie countered. She sat deep in thought for a moment. "Why do I need to know? Is he still a threat to me somehow?"

Jake hadn't really thought about it. He also hadn't expected Callie to be so prickly. "I just thought you would like to know, that's all."

"Does he know where to find you? Have you kept in touch?" Callie was curious and not ready to end the conversation just yet.

Jake too was eager to keep up the exchange. "I went to see him at the prison before that last day in your room in Seattle. He knows I live here. He also knows that I despise him and want nothing to do with him."

"Still, you're a doctor here, Jake. It won't be hard for him to find you if he wants to."

"Are you concerned about me?" Jake teased her, a tiny sample of the light banter they had always shared.

"I care, if that's what you're hinting about, Jake. You'll always be my first love; and it just so happens that the man we're talking about has a knack for torching buildings and people." Callie was serious, unwilling to let Jake resume the same lighthearted tone with her. She couldn't let him under her skin that far.

"My father wouldn't dare come after me. I've witnessed enough to put him away forever."

"That's exactly my point. Maybe he still thinks you'll try."

Perhaps it was his size, but Jake had never been easily intimidated. Still, a frisson of fear made it past his checkpoint and lodged itself in his gut. Could the old man still be that ballsy?

"You don't need to worry about me, Callie. You know I'm tough."

"But not bulletproof, Jake. Just promise me you'll watch your back."

"Not that you should read a bunch into this, but it does this heart a world of good to know that you still care," Jake said to Callie, as he stared at his hands.

"I can't help it." She paused. "I want you to know something else, Jake."

"What's that?"

"I understand why you didn't rat on your dad when you were a kid. I know what it's like to receive mercy in exchange for loyalty, how guilt can easily be mistaken for love. I've been there. I know you were as much your father's victim as I was."

Callie linked her hands with Jake's and brushed

each knuckle with her moist lips. Then she let him go and rose from the table. "Goodbye, Jake. Take care."

He had no words, so he simply nodded and watched her proud, slender back as she walked away from him for good.

V.J. watched the whole exchange from behind the travel guide stack. He'd been about to whisk Callie away for a late lunch when 'Jake the God' had walked through the door and straight to the window display. Out of respect for Callie's strength and her need for privacy, V.J. had tucked himself away, but kept a close eye on the situation should Dr. Jake get out of line.

She was about to streak right past him, tears in her eyes, purpose in her step when V.J. snaked out a hand to stop her. She let out a tiny hiccup of surprise, then seeing it was her friend, her face crumpled in unspent grief.

They stood together, V.J. comforting Callie, smoothing her hair, murmuring comfort words, until Callie regained her composure. One thing was sure—as ethereal as Callie could look, she was not a pretty crier. Her milky skin had become blotchy and her eyes red-rimmed.

"You look as if you've graced the canvas of an oil-painting and the artist accidentally smeared your entire face, Callie. Why don't you wipe away some of those tears." V.J. offered her his handkerchief.

"Th-thanks," she sup-supped between deep breaths. "I'm sorry. It's embarrassing to be so upset. Not very professional."

"Oh, Callie, we've moved way past all of that. You know I respect you as a professional. This is your friend V.J. now. I know you just walked away from Jake with the full intention of never turning around ever again, am I right?"

"I can't let him back in, V.J.. It would be like sleeping in the enemy camp."

"He can't help what his father did, Callie."

"Did I tell you that Jake was sitting in his father's truck when his father lit up our house?"

V.J. sighed. "I just cannot imagine what God was thinking putting you two, of all people, on a collision course."

Callie tried to lighten the mood. "Well at least Jake is available now. You should be thanking the Big Guy!"

"Well I'm not going to do that yet. I can't help believing that there is a purpose to all of this." V.J. wrung his hands, despair at Callie's situation gripping him.

"There is a purpose. Jake is a wonderful burn specialist. He ended up dedicating his life's work to helping people who've been victimized, much like we were. That's it, V.J.. I don't really fit into the equation."

"Except that here you are and you love him and he loves you and you are both being tortured all over again." V.J. looked into Callie's eyes, still brimming with unshed tears. "There is one more thing I must know, but only because I care about you so, Callie, dear."

"V.J., I would tell you anything. Even about this."

"You would tell me, but are you going to tell him?"

"Tell him what? What else is there to say?"

"Callie, are you planning to tell Jake that you're pregnant with his child?"

Suddenly the fatigue, the nausea, and her emotional distress all made perfect sense to Callie. She'd chalked her symptoms up to missing Jake. V.J. was keener than she, obviously. Because, without realizing it, she'd been missing something else also—her monthly cycle.

V.J. saw the confusion, the horror, and the wonder pass over Callie's face in barely more than an instant. She hadn't known. Maybe it was because he was gay and in touch with his feminine side, but V.J. could always tell when a woman was in a delicate state. He smiled now at Callie, encouraging her to be happy about her situation.

"But it was just a few weeks ago… I mean I'm barely…. How on Earth could you tell, V.J.?" Callie stammered, her face flushed.

"I have a gift. Just ask Shirley. I told her she'd conceived her little boy, Garrett, even before her little stick turned blue. Must be something in your aura."

Callie blanched briefly and sought a chair in the reading corner. "Oh, God, V.J.. I think you might be right. This is horrible."

"This is wonderful. You need only to decide what to tell Jake. The rest is up to you. For what it's worth, I know you'll be a fantastic mom."

Callie chewed her lower lip. This was somewhere on the cusp of the ultimate predicament. She'd thought she was walking away from Jake forever while her traitorous body conspired to bind him to her forever.

V.J. interrupted her reverie. "Well, whatever you must do, dear, I think it's best decided while your hands are busy. Have you seen our display window? Someone's made quite a mess! When it's finished, we'll get a bite to eat."

Callie laughed. V.J., ever the friend and boss—as she returned to designing her display she wondered what he would think of his new role: Godfather.

Chapter 28

Callie returned home at six that evening to find Leah intently watching the door, waiting for her on the sofa. Her first thought was that V.J. had called her and given her the news. But she knew V.J. would never have been so hasty.

There was definitely something wrong, though, because Leah was fidgeting, suddenly up on her crutches, fluffing pillows, straightening frames on the sofa table.

Leah turned her attention to Callie, worry lining her delicate features and clouding her sky blue eyes.

"How was your day at work?" She began.

"It was a little stranger than average. Jake stopped by today."

"Ooh, how did that go?" Leah was obviously skirting whatever was bothering her.

"He came to tell me that his father had gotten out of prison."

"Was he worried that his father might come after you?"

"How could he? I told him that his father would have no way of knowing my identity or location. He would, however, have no trouble finding Jake. Jake didn't seem worried, though."

"That's good. If he's not worried, then there is probably no reason to be," Leah reasoned.

"Why did he feel the need to come to me and tell

me then?"

"Maybe he just wanted to see you."

"There is that, I suppose," Callie demurred. Changing the subject because she could see that Leah was still obsessing about something, she spoke again.

"So are you going to tell me what's bothering you, Leah?"

"Oh, it's not much really. Just that Sean asked me to move in with him." Leah blushed and ducked her head.

"What? Oh my Gosh! That's great Leah. Really. You don't need to worry about me. I thought you'd be buying your own place soon anyway."

"I told him 'no.'" Leah gazed at her friend, her trepidation at her decision surfacing.

"You told him NO?" Callie couldn't believe it. Sean and Leah were so sweet together and she loved his parents and they had loved her. What could be so complicated as to make her say no?

"I've always promised myself, mostly, and my moms, that I wouldn't live with a guy before I married him." Leah replied, her resolve strong, but her heart weak with worry.

"That's noble and really not so old-fashioned, Leah. I can't imagine, the way Sean feels about you, that he would object to your reasoning."

"He didn't."

"So why are you so tense. I mean, good Lord, girl, you could bury a suitcase in those frown lines."

Leah laughed, though nervously. "Sean asked me to marry him instead."

The latest revelation prompted Callie to sit down. "And you said…."

"I didn't say no, but I did ask for time to think his proposal over."

"Are you crazy? Leah! How long did it take for you to finally land him in the first place? You two are so happy! Why wouldn't you say yes?"

Callie's tirade met Leah's exhausted worrying and all Leah could do was burst out in tears.

"I know," she said through her wet countenance, as Callie patted her back reassuringly. "I'm such a fool. It just seemed so sudden. I was taken by surprise. I don't know, Callie. I want to say yes. I do. What would you do?"

"Do you love him like I think you do?"

"I do, Callie. It's just been so fast. Sean's divorced. He may not take marriage as seriously as I do."

"His divorce is all the more reason he would never take proposing to you lightly," Callie countered. "He's been through the trenches of a failed marriage. He sees something in you that has reaffirmed his faith in the institution. You should be encouraged by this, not afraid of it."

"According to him, I am very different from his first wife."

"I should hope so."

"We have our work in common, too, so I understand the hours he dedicates to the hospital. That was a big problem for his socialite ex-wife."

"I can imagine. It's great for Sean that you understand his devotion to his work," Callie replied.

"Callie?"

"Yes, Leah?"

"What is my problem? I finally have the chance to be blissfully happy. I have the career I want and the man I want, and I seem determined to screw it up."

"You haven't screwed anything up, Leah. If Sean doesn't get this, then he doesn't get you. I bet he'll be happy to know that you've thought it over carefully."

"I need to find out."

"I'll call V.J. right now and arrange for him to take you over there in the Mercedes."

"I could take a bus."

"Are you kidding? You're on crutches. Let's get you to Nob Hill in style and as soon as possible."

The sparkle returned immediately to Leah's eyes. She was going to be engaged! She hobbled her spirited way to her room to change. Callie watched her go with a mixture of love and envy. If only it were so simple to figure out her own predicament.

*C*allie was to be the maid of honor with Filipa and Jolynn as bridesmaids. The date was set for April first. Leah thought the date appropriate given the tumultuous start she and Sean had gone through.

Callie only hoped that her figure would hold up to the lovely A-line periwinkle chiffon gowns Leah had picked out. The wedding date would put her pregnancy at four months according to the dates the doctor had given her.

So far Callie was holding only V.J. in her confidence. She didn't want to tell Leah about the baby because it would steal her wedding thunder. She wanted her friend to have every bit of attention she deserved on her special day.

Telling Jake was out of the question. Callie wasn't sure she could ever tell him about the baby. There was never any question in her mind about becoming a mother. She had been old enough to remember her own mother with her little sister Libby—the sweet embraces and smells of mother and child, as her mother bathed and nursed and rocked her. The coos and smiles of baby Libby and the wondrous laughs and gentle murmurs of her mother and father in response—all of it resonated in Callie's memory. She remembered the cocoon of warmth that had surrounded Libby and she knew innately that she and her brothers had enjoyed the same security.

Callie was intent on providing the same cloak of sanctuary for her own offspring. For years, Callie had struggled with the purpose, the reason for her life, when it had been so precariously held in the balance and her life had been fated to continue. Now she knew why she had been spared. She was meant to be a mother, to pass along her mother's green eyes and raven hair and her father's generous height and slender build.

This baby was already hers in all respects; and she embraced every wave of nausea, every moment that she fell mercifully asleep during her break or while she was reading a book or journaling. This pregnancy was her private joy. By the end of February, she was beginning to transform from looking wan and strained, to glowing.

She and Jake had talked about their future many times during their brief courtship, but they had never talked about having children. Jake focused on Callie and the travels and adventures they would have together. She'd always assumed the omission of children in their conversations was innocent on Jake's part, but now that she knew his family past, she realized that it was probably never his intention to procreate. When your mother abandoned you and your father spent your entire childhood burning down homes, churches, and barns before your very eyes, there was most definitely very little desire to further the gene pool.

As gentle and beautiful as Jake was, Callie didn't like to think about his genetic contribution to her baby. He'd had to work way too hard to shed his past. It's true that you don't choose your family, but those scary things about him, things he'd buried deep inside of him, worried her, so she put thoughts of these things aside.

It was almost as if, by hiding her pregnancy and her child from Jake, she could mentally deny that he was the baby's father. This baby would look like her, act like her, be like her—Callie's baby.

V.J., of course, was nonplussed that Callie wouldn't share her pregnancy with Jake. Ever a member of Jake's fan club, V.J. was convinced that Callie was selling him short. V.J. understood why Callie hadn't shared with Leah. As obsessed as the lovely woman was with her doctor fellow and her impending nuptials, V.J. doubted that Leah would be able to cope with the revelation anyway. He didn't, and wouldn't ever, justify Callie's neglect of Jake. It was pure ignorance and fear that drove her. He could only hope she would come to her senses.

*J*ake started to live again. He was thrilled for Leah and excited about her wedding and one positive thing that had come from wallowing over Callie was the friendship that had evolved with Lanny. They had their bachelorhood in common and Lanny was a good guy, a Southern gentleman, with values similar to Jake.

He could talk to Lanny for hours (usually at some sort of watering hole) and never feel the need to say something deep or profound. They were just guys being guys. They flirted plenty with the opposite sex, though Lanny was the only one who felt the need to take anyone home. Being friends with Lanny was very much like his friendship with Bob. There were no strings, no expectations, just companionship, someone to hang with. Jake was grateful for the company.

He still missed Callie with an ache like an ulcer in the pit of his stomach. He wondered constantly how she was and he wished her silently well. Alas, life kept moving. He kept saving lives and healing morbidly burned children and adults. He played Frisbee in the park with Bob. He did small projects around the house and he went out frequently in the evenings with Lanny.

Jake was pretty sure he would never fall in love

again. The love of his life wanted nothing to do with him. He didn't have the heart to try again. So he tried to take pleasure in the parts of his life that had once meant so much to him—before Callie. There would be an 'after Callie,' if only he was patient; if only it didn't rip him apart to know he needed to move on.

Chapter 29

April first dawned to a blanket of fog that dissipated at precisely noon. Leah and Sean O'Carroll descended the steps of the cathedral at four p.m. amidst a gaggle of soapy bubbles irridescing in the sun. The only things brighter than the afternoon were their smiles.

Callie and Jake stole glances at each other as she faced the crowd with the wedding party. Her face had gotten fuller and she'd gained weight, mostly in her chest, but the gown flowed flawlessly around her only slightly swollen belly. Elegant, loose-fitting chiffon sleeves covered her unsightly arm and torso. She resembled a medieval maiden with violets and baby's breath woven through her cascading hair. She looked healthy, radiant, and the periwinkle set off her verdant eyes. Jake's heart lurched at the sight of her.

He let his hair get longer and it curled on his broad shoulders. He looked like Matthew McConaughey, just as strapping, just as sexy, only with eyes the inviting color of the Caribbean. Jake's eyes. Callie's heart did a little flutter of its own and she stilled it in time to feel another tickle low in her gut, as though her baby knew Callie had just laid her gaze on his or her daddy.

Leah and Sean were whisked away in a white limousine to their waterfront reception and Callie rode with one of the groomsmen in his Bentley. She and Jake had no time to talk either before or during the reception. She and Killian, the best man and Sean's brother, had put together a short and sweet rhyme for their toast and she had begged off dancing after their first couple of tribute dances to the newlyweds.

Jake knew Callie was busy in her role as maid of honor, but it was also obvious that she was avoiding him. He took her cue and left with Lanny shortly after the festivities turned from wedding traditions to an all-out dance party. It was just too hard to be so near her again and not want to invite her into his arms.

Callie sensed when Jake left the reception room without even looking around. It was like someone flipped off a switch. She looked at V.J. and he nodded sadly, admonishing her in his way. She sighed in relief. She would have no reason to see Jake at all now. She might never have to tell him he was going to be a father. The flutter in her belly objected and she ran to the bathroom to be sick.

*C*onfession lightens the soul. Telling Leah and Cyrus about her pregnancy relieved Callie almost enough to make her believe she had it made. They were, of course, thrilled for her, despite her reluctance to admit paternity.

She and V.J. moved her things into Leah's bedroom and she donned a gas mask and painted and wallpapered the baby's room. V.J. bought her a lovely maple crib and Callie took a class in knitting so she could make infant caps and booties and blankets for her fall arrival.

V.J. attended her ultrasound with her and they laughed as the baby kicked out a tune and shifted repeatedly in and out of the view of the sonographer. He or she was already a little athlete. Callie refused to know the gender, choosing neutral colors in clothes and accessories, and waiting for the surprise that only God and time would reveal.

The baby became increasingly active and Callie became more physically sluggish, but she never felt so energized as she did in her sixth month. She knew that V.J. would kill her if he could see her, but she just had to move the bookcase and the sofa table around anyway. She was in the throes of sorting through her book collection when her apartment buzzer rang.

She frowned. She wasn't expecting anyone. It was a sunny June afternoon and she was wearing a halter tank top with hip hugger maternity shorts to stay cool while she worked. Her black hair was pulled off her face in a careless ponytail. She had on no makeup. She glanced at the hall mirror. Every scar on her chest and arm was apparent. Yep, she looked scary. The buzzer rang again for emphasis.

She hit the intercom.

"Yes?"

"I'm looking for Callie Justice. Is this Callie?" It was a woman's voice, but not one she recognized. She sounded older, her voice nervous and high-pitched, like a warbler.

"Can I ask who you are?" Callie replied, cautious about letting a stranger through, female or not.

"My name is Felicia King. My maiden name is Shepherd. You might recognize that name. Wesley Shepherd is my brother. Jacob Shepherd Lamb is my nephew."

Jake's aunt. Callie shuddered. What could this woman possibly want with her and how did she get her address?

"Can I help you, Ms. King?"

"Could you possibly let me in, Callie? So we can talk face to face? I'm not used to this whole intercom business. We're small town people."

She sounded innocent enough, but for all Callie knew she was built like a Sumo wrestler. Besides, Callie was hardly in any shape to receive, of all people, a relative of Jake's.

"I'm sorry, Ms. King. I can't let you in. I'm not properly dressed…"

"Oh, dear, I see," Felicia King replied. "That is disappointing. You see I got your address from your father, Cyrus. Greta Lamb put me in touch with him. He was quite convinced that I would do you no harm."

"Cyrus sent you?" Callie was confused. Her father was nothing short of protective of her, especially now. This must be important.

"That's right. Cyrus thought you might want to hear from me." Felicia was encouraged.

"Hold on. I'll buzz you through." Against her better judgment, but with her curiosity getting the best of her, Callie let the woman through and swiftly disappeared to her room to grab a roomy sweatshirt.

Felicia knocked lightly at the door when she'd ascended the steps. Callie opened the door to a portly, winded woman in an *Alcatraz* sweatshirt. She wore her white hair in an old-fashioned bun on the top of her head and her jean shorts hung loosely around spindly legs that belied the rest of her build. Only her eyes betrayed her relationship to Jake.

"Welcome to San Francisco, Felicia. I see you've already seen one of our more infamous attractions," Callie quipped and opened her door to her guest.

"Actually, Jake sent me this years ago. I figured it would make me blend in with the rest of the tourists." The warm smile and twinkle in Felicia King's eyes reminded Callie so much of Jake that she chided herself for not letting the poor woman in the door in the first place. This woman meant Callie no harm.

Callie relaxed. When she took a deep breath and turned around, she heard Felicia pause and take in a quick breath.

"Is there something wrong?" Callie inquired.

"Oh dear, Callie. Cyrus didn't tell me you were expecting. I didn't realize you had gotten married and settled quite so soon after Jake…."

Callie chuckled lightly at Felicia's discomfort. She decided that what the woman didn't know could never harm either of them. "Felicia, don't you know? You don't have to be married nowadays. Somehow a baby just jumped right in there."

"Of course. I didn't mean…" Felicia shifted uncomfortably.

"It's okay. Really. I get used to the assumptions," Callie replied warmly. "Why don't you come in and have a seat on the sofa. I have some herbal apple cinnamon tea on the stove. I can heat it up if you'd like some."

"That would be very nice. Thank you." Felicia admired the sunny apartment as she made her way in and sat down at the kitchen bar instead of the sofa.

"It looks like you've been nesting, honey," she observed.

"Is that what you'd call it? It just seems like the weekend beckons with another project the minute I've already finished one."

"Everything needs to be just so?" Felicia asked knowingly.

"Exactly." She liked this woman.

"Besides Jake, I raised three boys of my own," Felicia shared, "I'd guess that's what you're having also. Do you know if you'll have a girl or a boy?"

Callie eased into conversation with Felicia about the baby, showing her the nursery, almost forgetting who Felicia was. But there was that issue—why was she here?

As if reading her mind, or perhaps sensing Callie's hesitation, Felicia suddenly asked, "I suppose you're wondering why I'm here?"

"Yes. You could say that. Jake and I split quite some time ago."

"Jake won't take my calls anymore, nor heed my warnings. I decided that you, his old flame, might know some way to get through to the stubborn young lout."

"He's in danger?" Callie tried to be casual, but she was alarmed anyway.

"You know, I'm not sure. All I know is this: My brother came to stay with me in January after his release from prison. Callie, I know he's done terrible things to you and your family, but he's my brother. He needed a place to stay. I offered. Maybe he's been reformed." She paused as if trying to convince herself once again.

"Yet here you are," Callie interrupted. "He ran off, didn't he?"

"He left a note in May. Said he had unfinished business in the Bay Area."

Callie shivered again despite her warm sweatshirt. "He wouldn't know about me or where I live, Felicia. How could I be unfinished business? Why are you and Jake so insistent that I might be in danger?"

"Callie, honey. I'm not worried about you. I only looked you up because Jake wrote me back and told me about you and your family after I told him Wes was out of prison. I read between the lines that he loved you. I could tell he was heartbroken, but I could also tell he had very little regard for the danger his father might put him in. He said his mother knew about you. I've corresponded for years with Greta about Jake, at her request. I looked you up for Jake's sake.

"Do you still care about him, Callie?" Felicia probed, her eyes earnest, worried for her nephew as she would be for one of her own sons.

"I'll always care about Jake." It was a fact, Callie knew.

"His father is going to hurt him, isn't he?" She

asked resignedly.

"You know, I don't know. I do want Jake watching his back, though. Wes is here in San Francisco somewhere and you and I know what he is capable of. He did seem remorseful, pensive, while he was with me. I didn't detect any malice. But here's the rub—if you had asked me twenty years ago if my brother was capable of the destruction he'd inflicted on people, I would have called you crazy. Wes may well be a sociopath. Or he could just be trying to cultivate a relationship with his son."

"How can I help, Felicia?" Callie was intensely worried about Jake, but she didn't know how she could possibly help his aunt without revealing to Jake her most precious secret.

"I don't want to put you in any jeopardy, Callie. You are safest here. Wesley doesn't even really know you exist or that you have any importance to him. Let's keep it that way. But can you speak to Jake, Callie?"

"And tell him what?" Callie worried her lower lip with her teeth.

"I'm in town to look for my brother and I'm going to try and find him and what he's up to before he can make any kind of move on Jake. I need you to convince my stubborn nephew that he needs to take cover, to possibly move for a few months and to keep a low profile until we know he's safe. Maybe he could stay here with you?"

Callie felt her blood run cold. That would be the last thing on Earth she'd want to do. He'd see the nursery, her belly. He would know. He couldn't know.

"Oh dear, I've upset you." Felicia apologized, patting Callie's arm, examining her worrisome pallor.

What an impossible choice. Either she made a move to try and protect the man she, Lord help her, still loved and the father of her child, and blew her cover. Or she continued fooling herself into believing she didn't care and let the man who terrorized her family hurt someone else she loved.

In her heart, there wasn't really a choice to make. Callie knew exactly what she had to do. She laid her hand over the top of Felicia's and nodded bravely.

Chapter 30

They spent the evening making plans. Callie invited Felicia to stay for dinner and Callie made them a smoked salmon and sun-dried tomato fettucine accompanied by crusty Italian bread from the delicatessen two blocks away. Never fond of wine, Felicia joined Callie in toasting to Jake's safety over a tall glass of skim milk.

The two chatted like old friends. Felicia offered advice and told amusing stories from her sons' babyhoods. Callie confessed Jake's paternity over their dessert of strawberries and marbled pound cake. Felicia took the admission in stride. She'd done the math already, owing to Callie's size and due date, and the date of Jake's letter.

Felicia was conservative in her small-town way, but she was completely supportive of Callie and her decision to raise her child with or without his father's help. She also gave loving testament to Jake's capacity to be a father, telling her stories of a strapping youth with enormous emotional scars, but a determination to rise above and to embrace life with humor and empathy.

Felicia wasn't pushy or presumptive and she liked Callie as much as Callie liked her. Callie was wise beyond her years and she would make the right decision.

Sensing Felicia's support, reinforcing her decision

to talk to Jake and coerce him into hiding from his father, Callie imagined that this was what it would be like to have her own mother around—she felt supported and persuaded all at the same time.

Callie also knew what an incredible gift Jake and V.J. had given her, making her look past her physical imperfections and her destructive introspection long enough to open herself to new people. She had a newfound ability to make friends and she now counted Felicia King as one of them.

It was nearly ten o'clock by the time Callie looked at the clock on her DVD player and realized how late it had gotten. Beulah, whom Callie had kept after Leah moved in with Sean and his cat-hating dogs, was perched lazily across her lap. Her sudden exclamation sent the feline flying off her lap.

"Oh my! I've been jabbering so much I didn't realize what time it was!" Beulah fixed Callie with a disdainful glare.

"It got dark on us, Felicia. How did you get here?"

"I took a taxi. I can't say I've been brave enough in the past two days to attempt the Bay Area Transit System. There are more people and buses here than in the whole State of Washington!"

"I believe that. I remember how daunting it can be. Do you need to stay here for the night?" Callie offered, not at all uncomfortable to have this sweet old lady stay with her.

"I couldn't, Callie, but it is lovely of you to offer. I don't even have my beauty kit," Felicia patted her neat bun subconsciously.

"Can I at least call you a taxi?"

"That would be useful. I'll use the powder room in the meantime."

While Felicia took herself off to the bathroom, Callie called V.J. and told him her plans to meet with

Jake in the early morning at the end of his all-night shift. Then she begged a favor and, ever so fond of his white Mercedes, begged him to break it out of the garage once more to deliver her new friend to her hotel.

V.J. was willing to do anything to help the woman who had finally brought Callie to her senses. He traded his turquoise silk pajamas for a jogging suit and hustled over to Callie's.

Felicia and Callie parted with a hug and a promise to meet the next day for lunch. Felicia would spend the morning scouring shelters and soup kitchens for any sign of Wesley. Callie would do her best to persuade Jake to hide, even if it meant him moving in with her.

Callie fell into bed, her nerves too frayed to invite sleep, but her taxed body too exhausted to stave it off.

Chapter 31

*T*he homeless man wondered whether there would be room at the shelter that night, or if he would find a cardboard box in the alley behind the department store again. The prison paid a pittance for the physical labor he did—mending fences, digging ditches, and basically breaking his aging back. He was able to afford cheap motels when he came to San Francisco, but the money ran out. Now he had just enough for one hot meal a day and he begged another from a local soup kitchen.

This trip had a purpose. He had found the man he was looking for, but he had yet to find the courage to approach him.

How did you tell your son you were sorry, knowing you failed him in every fundamental way? When his wife left, he held his infant son in his arms and promised to fulfill his every dream, to make his life successful and happy. He was pretty sure his son had such a life, despite his father's mistakes.

When the urge struck to build a fire, to see it burn, to feel the power, the control, he tried to shelter his son from it. He was so careful not to wake him when putting him in the truck. He'd never awaken his son to witness the deeds that fed his demented soul. He had also been very careful to never get caught, so he wouldn't have to leave his son.

He himself had been left so many times. First by his father, then by the many mates that his mother chose, the last being the one who introduced him to fire—lighters, matches, cigarettes, fuel—sometimes on piles of wood or garbage, sometimes on his skin, when he crossed the evil man. He kept his little sister as far away from his mom's lovers as possible and he sheltered her from this one too. His sister never abandoned him, even now, and he loved her for it.

His wife was the last to leave him and the loss snapped his self-control entirely. Nobody else would ever leave his son; but he failed at that too. He was imprisoned and he cost his son a woman he cared about, if what his sister said was true.

He was going to make it up to him, though, if it took his last breath to do it. He already knew where his son worked, where he lived. He fought the madness that still spoke to him, urging him to make fire, to do what came easiest and brought the most satisfaction to him. He buried the urges as deeply as they would go. He would not hurt his son or his sister again. He huddled in the evening chill, wondering where to go for the night, wondering when absolution would come to him.

Chapter 32

The bars closed that early Sunday morning at two o'clock. The barkeeps wiped down their counters, swept their floors and drug themselves home to their beds. The city slept, excepting for the few transients wandering the early summer streets and the teenagers sowing their oats and necking in the parks.

It was the San Andreas Fault that awoke first that morning, rousing San Francisco from its sleepy shroud and tipping its residents on their ears. The fracture came from deep within the earth in the middle of the Bay and sent it's shockwaves through tunnels and bridges, upsetting the foundations of buildings, hurtling about the furnishings and valuables of most of the Bay Area residents.

Callie's eyes snapped open at the sound of an ear-popping crack and she was five years old once again, her slumber slaughtered by the panic of a dire emergency. She had the presence of mind to weave across the swaying room to her bedroom doorway and to hang on as the pictures lining her hallway swung on their hooks, several falling to the floor with a jagged crash.

Her stucco building suffered several cracks in its half-century of existence from other tremblers, but it was built with shifting earth in mind and, after the initial shaking of the earthquake, Callie was relieved to find sturdy floors still under her feet. Nonetheless, she threw on some clothes, chucked wide-eyed Beulah into her cat carrier, and packed a knapsack with bottled water, protein bars, a change of clothes, and a toothbrush. She needed to get to V.J. and then to the hospital to see if Leah, Sean, and Jake were okay and if she could do anything to help them with casualties.

Shaky, but with adrenaline fueling her progress, Callie took the stairs to ground floor. There were ugly gashes in the usually pristine hallway plaster, but really her building looked surprisingly intact.

An alarming number of San Franciscans had hit the streets in their bedraggled panic. Callie pushed through the crowds of people to get to V.J.'s penthouse apartment just five blocks from work. This meant she would have to hoof at least seventeen blocks with her increasingly awkward body.

She passed by the store, and noted that *Victorian Juxtapositions* fared less well than her apartment building. Callie could see, in the early morning light, that the window display was a jumbled mess and the leaded glass window had massive cracks in it. There were pieces missing from the gingerbread lattice and, as she peered inside, she could see the stacks had thrown books helter-skelter.

Aware of the work V.J. and the rest of them would have to do to put the store back together, Callie was bolstered further into finding her friends and pitching in to help where she could in the path of destruction. She was weaving through people on her way to V.J.'s when the man himself plucked her out of the crowd and gave her a breath-stealing hug.

"Oh, Thank God, Callie. I was just on my way to your place. You look okay. In fact, you look fantastic considering the rather abrupt awakening we've all gotten." V.J. hugged her once more then released her and peered into Beulah's carrier.

"Hello, Miss," he said affectionately. "I see you're

unscathed also." He smiled at Callie and she noticed that he was wearing the same jogging suit he had on the night before. His pale blond hair stood on end.

"Have you been by the store yet, V.J.?"

"Not yet. I was headed straight for your place after I made sure my apartment was secure. Looters will be out in full force before too long. Don't forget, I was here for the big 1989 quake. This was just a gentle shake compared to that one, but desperately scared people can do desperately stupid things, believe me.

"I take it you've seen the store?" V.J. continued, concern lining his features. He had quite a lot on his plate, being responsible for four retail establishments, as well as his home.

"It's a mess, V.J., but nothing we can't tackle or fix. It's standing. That's the important thing."

"Well, it is an old house, dating well before both of the big quakes and the fires. It's withstood much worse than this. I'll get there eventually. I hardly know where to start assessing damage. I was coming to find you to see if you needed anything. You are more delicate, and important, after all, than any old building."

Callie cradled V.J.'s face in her hand. "I'm glad you're okay too, my friend."

"Can I do anything for you, Callie?"

"Actually, I was hoping you could give me a ride to *St. Katherine's*. Jake's shift should just be getting over and I'm sure he'll be there receiving casualties. I would expect Leah and Sean to go there straight away also. I thought I'd see if I could help."

"And see if they're all okay, too?"

She nodded solemnly. V.J. grabbed the cat carrier and they started back toward his building together. "Traffic's going to be a bear," he said. "But we'll have a much better shot in my car than we would have on public transportation."

"Thanks, V.J.." Callie gripped his hand.

"Don't mention it, kid. Why don't we leave Beulah at my apartment? She probably wouldn't be very welcome at the hospital."

Callie's brow furrowed with her intense need to see the other people she cared about. They couldn't get to the hospital soon enough.

St. Katherine's was in ordered chaos. Nurses took charge triaging the many less seriously injured patients and security kept a tight reign over the happenings. Callie and V.J. were allowed into the facility after Jolynn, who was handling pediatric injuries, recognized Callie and asked security to send her through.

"Callie. Are you injured?" Jolynn was quick to look Callie over. "Is the baby okay?"

"Oh, yes. He seems to be just fine. He's moving around a lot, as excited as everyone else is, apparently. I'm really just here to see if Leah and Sean are here and if they're okay," Callie replied, not wanting to delay Jolynn, but anxious to see her friends. All the while, she scanned the emergency area to see if she could get a glimpse of Jake. By now, it was seven a.m. and the morning shift had joined the night shift. The staff was busy, but not overwhelmed.

Callie's attention came back to Jolynn, who had begun to tell her where she could find Leah.

"… and Sean are tending to the patients with obvious fractures. They're on the second floor between Rehab and Diagnostic Imaging."

"Thanks, Jolynn. I'll come back to see if there's anything I can do after I've talked to them."

"That's sweet of you, Callie, but we're doing alright here. The injuries are mostly bruises and cuts. People are just trickling in at this point. We could arrange an ultrasound when you get back if you like, just to see if the baby's okay."

"It's very sweet of you to offer. I might take you up on that later," Callie replied.

She bid Jolynn goodbye and V.J. accompanied her to the second floor, where they asked the Rehab secretary, who recognized Callie, where they could find Sean or Leah.

They were pointed toward the Imaging reading area where Sean O'Carroll was examining x-rays and a CAT scan.

"Sean."

"Oh, hi Callie. It's a relief to see you. Are you and 'Junior' doing okay?" Sean had loosened up so much since he and Leah's blossoming romance that even the most adversarial coworkers had to admit to the improvement. Even in the midst of crisis, his demeanor was serious, but light and he gave Callie a brief hug.

"We're fine. How are you and Leah?"

"We were getting up and getting our coffee when our mugs shook clean off the countertop."

"Is your house still standing?" V.J. inquired.

"Yeah. A few vases and picture frames and dishes were broken, but the only thing truly ruined was our day of golf in Sonoma County."

"So much for Sunday being our day of rest," Leah quipped as she walked into the reading room behind them.

She and Callie embraced and Leah held her friend at arm's length to see the strain etching Callie's face. "It's going to be all right, kiddo," Leah said lightly as she put her arm back around her friend.

"I'm just happy to see you both." Her worry for just one more person remained unspoken.

Knowingly, Leah asked, "Have you gone by to see Jake yet?"

"I was supposed to go to his house and meet with him after his shift. His aunt says that he's working graveyard shifts now."

"Yeah. We sure miss him at lunch nowadays," Leah lamented.

"So is he downstairs somewhere?" Callie asked.

"No. He didn't work last night. We expected him to come in because they've called all staff in to help with the influx of casualties, but we haven't seen him yet."

"I thought he was working…" Callie's mouth suddenly went dry. Anxiety had been niggling at her since the earthquake. She hadn't recognized its source. Jake. He was in trouble.

Leah saw the dread fill Callie's face. "I'm sure he's fine, Callie. He's probably on his way here now." She tried to soothe her friend. This kind of stress wasn't good for her or the baby.

"V.J., why don't you take Callie over to Jake's. It's only a quarter mile from here. I'm sure she'll feel better if she can see him," Leah suggested.

"I'll give you directions," Callie offered, in a hurry to do just that. She kissed Leah on the cheek. "I'm sure you're right, Leah. He's probably just fine. But I bet Bob's having a tizzy."

Leah's laugh sounded as tinny as the taste in Callie's mouth.

Chapter 33

*I*n Pacific Heights, the daylight revealed stately mansions with damaged bricks and porticos, fortresses whose occupants remained in their confines. The radio reported the heaviest damage from a 5.0 earthquake in the areas closest to the water in Marin County and in the Chinatown and Union Square Districts of San Francisco. Most roads were passable, but the announcer advised people to stay home if at all possible to stave off chaos in public places and to prevent looting.

The governor declared a state of emergency in the Bay Area and troops were en route to the city to keep order. Callie and V.J. absorbed all of this even as Callie's panic rose to her throat, threatening to choke her. Jake should have been at the hospital. Something was wrong.

She could see the smoke from three blocks away, billowing black against the perfect dawn, and Callie knew instantly that it was Jake's home that was on fire. V.J. sensed her urgency, even as he tried to reassure her. He pressed increasingly harder on the accelerator and prayed that she was wrong.

Three homes were alight, with Jake's at the center of the rowhouses. A crowd gathered around and V.J. heard the roar of approaching fire trucks. The blaze was furiously eating up the structures and the whole block was in danger of igniting. V.J. got as close as he could to the fray and parked the Mercedes. He expected Callie to bolt from the car, but instead she sat transfixed, her mouth working in silent terror, her eyes reflecting clearly from their green depths that her psyche had leapt completely to another moment in time.

V.J. didn't know what to do, so lost and frightened was Callie's soul. He went to her side of the car and leaned in front of her, looking into her eyes, imploring her to come back to him. She blinked once, twice.

"Callie. Callie. Oh, honey, you must answer me. We have to find Jake. Come back to me so that we can find Jake."

"Libby. Timothy. Jamie. Oh God. Mommy. Daddy. MOMMY? DADDY?" She chanted.

"JAKE, Callie. We need to find JAKE." V.J. shook her shoulders gently.

"Jake?" Callie broke briefly from her reverie.

"Yes, Callie. Jake. His home is involved in a fire, but I'm sure he's okay. We need to look for him."

"Jake? V.J.? OH MY GOD! V.J.! WE HAVE TO FIND JAKE!"

"That's my girl. Let's get out and go find Jake," V.J. soothed. He was no longer certain he should have brought Callie here, but he was grateful she'd emerged from that frightening trance.

Callie exited the car shakily, the smell of smoke engulfing her. She fought back despair and a wave of nausea once more. She laid a hand on her active fetus as if to soothe him or her. She spoke quietly, her strength kicking in, "Come on, Baby. Let's go find your daddy."

In a sea of faces, the first that she recognized was Felicia's. She looked around her to see if Jake was nearby, to no avail. The two women embraced and the fear between them remained unspoken. Jake's townhome sat on a gentle slope and they stood on the sidewalk across from it. The flames licked the formerly graceful framework of the antique homes. The roar of fire engines drowned out the voice of the fire.

"I heard the neighbors say maybe there was some sort of gas leak after the quake…" Felicia began, yelling above the din.

Callie stood in stony silence, certain that an inferno had swallowed yet another of her loved ones.

V.J. asked what all of them were thinking. "Where is your brother, Felicia?"

"I don't know," she wailed, hysteria setting in. "I didn't have time to find him. He couldn't… Please, no. Wesley. Jake." Felicia fell to her knees.

Callie simply stared ahead, mesmerized by the beauty and revulsion of the burning buildings. Movement from behind a second floor window broke through her reverie once again. She saw a flash of red. Bob. It was Bob inside the house! She yelled his name. Was Jake in there too?

An antique wooden chair came crashing through the living room window and muscle-laden arms cleared away the jagged glass and thrust the bloodhound through into the fresh air, dropping him onto the porch roof below, from which Bob leapt to safety and immediately turned his face back toward the window, barking furiously, seeking his master.

To Callie's complete horror, Jake stood outlined in the window for barely a heartbeat before he collapsed. The man she loved, the father of her unborn child, disappeared, out of sight, and forever out of reach, as his home burned down around him.

Chapter 34

The fire trucks arrived and the alarm was sounded: A man had briefly appeared in the second floor window of the middle house. All other occupants of the three houses had escaped unharmed. Callie watched numbly while the firemen positioned the ladder truck and the tanker truck hooked up to the nearest hydrant and began to pour water over the maelstrom.

Minutes passed that felt like hours when suddenly a broad, tall man donning a trench coat, curly white hair cascading past his shoulders, bolted past fire officials, stealthily kicked down the front door and disappeared into a fog of smoke and steam. A fireman started after him, but the chief rushed to hold him back. It was too dangerous. Let the ladder truck do its job.

Like an apparition, the trench-coated figure appeared silhouetted in the open window, his clothing aflame, bearing a load almost his size in a wool blanket. He dragged the bundle across the sill and it slithered heavily over the portico to the concrete driveway below.

Precisely two breaths later, the top two floors of the town home caved in, just as the ladder was approaching the window. The ladder operator steered the firemen quickly away from the collapsing structure.

Helpless to do anything about the man in the trenchcoat, the firemen nevertheless worked steadily to continue to drench what was left of the home.

Paramedics rushed to the aid of the man who was

dropped from the second story window.

It was Jake. He was unconscious, but breathing fresh air. He was rushed to an ambulance and put on oxygen. Paramedics were looking him over for burns, only to find that the blanket had staved off the most intense heat. Jake thought he'd died and gone to heaven when he opened his eyes and saw Callie's face directly above his, her ebony hair ringed in light from the overheads in the ambulance. She was crying.

"Did somebody die?" He croaked, his trademark humor cutting through the intensity of the moment.

"Not you, Jake. Thank God. Not you," was Callie's reply and she kissed him with her soft ruby lips and sat back to take a ride with Jake to the hospital.

V.J. scooped Felicia off the ground, grabbed Bob by the collar, then put them both in the car and followed the ambulance to the hospital. Callie needed a ride and Jake needed all of them.

Felicia was babbling, still in shock at the turn of events. Only Bob was truly calm. He sat like a sentinel on the back seat, his huge red head poised between them. His best friend was in the vehicle in front of them and they were headed the right direction.

V.J. steered into the emergency entrance at *St. Katherine's*, parking tickets be damned, and ushered Felicia and Bob into the emergency area.

The security guard spoke up, "I'm sorry, you can't bring that dog…"

"Good sir," V.J. interrupted. "Dr. Jake Lamb was just brought in here and this is his best friend, Bob. Do you know Dr. Lamb?"

The guard stammered, "I do. He's a great guy. It's just…"

"Dr. Lamb almost died getting this animal to safety. Do you really want to stand between them now?"

"No, sir."

"Very well, then," V.J. concluded as he and Felicia and Bob continued past the gaping guard.

Jake's stretcher was paused at the entrance to the first treatment bay and Bob went straight to him and, settling on his hind legs, very gently put his paws on the edge of the stretcher and pulled himself up to meet Jake's eyes. Callie looked on, smiling her approval. Jake reached up with both arms, wincing at the effort, and embraced his loyal pooch. They stayed like that for a while.

When Bob finally got down, even the nurses were misty-eyed. Jake's eyes filled with questions when he returned his focus to Callie.

"You saved him, Jake," she said gently, her voice full of admiration.

"I couldn't leave him behind," Jake's voice sounded as if he'd swallowed a truckload of gravel.

"I know. You love him and you laid down your own life for him. That's why I'm putting my money on you."

"I hope it's a safe bet, because you know I abhor gambling," Jake teased.

"I bet you'll make a wonderful father," Callie said softly, seriously, smiling deep into Jake's azure orbs.

Jake swept his gaze over Callie as realization dawned. His face lit with unadulterated joy. "Well, now, Callie, I think I'd like to put some money on that too."

V.J. and Felicia sat in the emergency waiting room, waiting for Jake to be x-rayed and examined. He was stable, though, and it appeared that he was out of danger from the smoke inhalation.

Felicia was still overcome by emotion and V.J. left her to her own thoughts as he reflected on the events of the morning. Injured San Franciscans were still appearing steadily at the doors of *St. Katherine's* and the waiting room was veritably overflowing with patients and their families.

Leah sent a volunteer to get Bob and take him to their place, where he could visit with his 'girls.' V.J. finally roused Felicia and invited her to the cafeteria to get coffee and cinnamon rolls. She followed robotically and V.J. began to slowly coax her out of her shock.

"Would you like cream and sugar, Felicia?"

"What? Oh. Cream, please," she responded.

"Would you like a roll with raisins or without?"

"With, please." She obediently followed V.J. with his tray to a table nearby.

He let her sip at her coffee for a while, watched the warmth bring some color back to her pale skin. He didn't know this woman, but she'd clearly been traumatized by all that had happened to her nephew.

"Are you feeling better now, Felicia?"

"I'm starting to get the feeling back in my fingers and toes. I think I was forgetting to breathe for a while there," she admitted, embarrassed at her behavior.

"Don't be ashamed, dear. For a few precious moments, I was sure we'd lost Jake too."

"Just think how Callie felt, watching the father of her child collapse like that," Felicia replied.

"So she told you the 'Great White Secret.'" V.J. feigned surprise, though he knew Callie had taken to Felicia immediately.

"It wasn't hard to deduce, V.J.. It took Jake exactly one split second to figure it out also."

"I'm so relieved that he knows now," V.J. replied.

"Me too. He's been liberated in every way today, hasn't he?" Felicia said pensively.

"How do you mean?" V.J. missed her reasoning.

"There aren't any secrets, no more surprises awaiting him. He was saved and he was told the truth."

"He also lost all of his worldly possessions," V.J.

observed.

"And he lost his father," Felicia said calmly, certain that she was right, as sadness overcame her features.

"The man in the trench coat..." V.J. began.

"I'm sure it was Wesley. His hair was long and white like that when he was released from prison. I didn't recognize the jacket, but I did recognize the build, the way he moved. He saved Jake's life."

"And lost his own. You don't think he set the fire, do you?" V.J. watched her carefully.

"No. The neighbors seemed fairly certain that the fire was secondary to the gas leak from the earthquake. Wesley came in time to finally take care of his son, not to hurt him again."

"I believe you are right, Felicia. Will you tell Jake?"

"In time, V.J.. I'll get the dental records for the police—make sure—and then I'll tell him."

"I'm sorry that you lost your brother today."

She began to cry softly. "So am I. But I'm happy too—that he finally found salvation, a way to atone for his sins, a way to make peace with himself and with Jake."

V.J. took her hand on the tabletop and they sat that way for the longest time, she in her grief and he in his infinitely graceful way of understanding just the right thing to do in any situation.

Chapter 35

*J*ake didn't exactly escape unscathed. The fall from the porch roof broke his ankle and fractured three of his ribs. Callie turned out to be the perfect analgesic. She hardly left his side for his first few days in the hospital. His ordeal left him sleepy and disoriented, but thankfully not seriously burned.

She watched him sleep; and when he was awake and able to talk, Callie confessed her continuing love and how miserable she was without him. She apologized that it had taken nearly losing him for her to see the light. She also admitted her intention to tell him about the baby the very morning that Mother Nature threw their lives into upheaval.

The fire marshall pinpointed the cause of the fire as a break in the natural gas line leading to the houses, secondary to the earthquake. Residents had smelled gas shortly before the explosion and they turned out to be correct. On his third day in the hospital, the medical examiner officially confirmed that the man who died in Jake's house fire was, in fact, Wesley Shepherd.

Jake took in this information with very little surprise. He imagined it was his father's strong arms that held him as he took him from the smoke and flame-filled room. It felt like the times his father would pluck him, sound asleep, from his bed at midnight or later to take him in the truck to set a fire. He'd scoop him up in his strong arms, in a blanket, and throw him like a sack of potatoes across the truck seat. Jake fell further this time, but that was the only sensation that was different.

He had hated his father for so long that regret took some time to settle in and then he allowed himself to feel it. His father had brought him life twice and as soon as he married Callie—she wasn't about to get away again—Jake would make sure he lived it to its fullest.

Felicia returned to Washington with Wesley's ashes where she would memorialize him by spreading them in the mountains around Goldendale, where they grew up.

Sean O'Carroll set Jake's ankle and Leah Westfield-O'Carroll fitted him with a wrap she'd designed for football players with bruised ribs.

Callie graciously offered to have Jake stay with her until he could replace his home and possessions.

Bob was staying with Sean and Leah until Jake could find or build a new home. The apartment was simply too small for Beulah and a cat-curious bloodhound. Jake had nothing to move into Callie's, but she shopped for clothing and toiletries, including replicas of his favorite bathrobe and slippers. Even his favorite brand of chinos hung on 'his' side of the closet, waiting for him to get well enough to go back to work.

Jake worried whether his first night in Callie's abode would be awkward for both of them. After all, both of them had always been on their own, sharing a bed on occasional nights, but never a home. Callie made a delicious Caesar and grilled chicken salad for them both, with lots of parmesan, and they plopped in front of the T.V. to watch a rerun of ER.

Setting his plate on the coffee table, marveling again at Callie's talent in the kitchen, Jake leaned back into the sofa and sighed, stretching his muscled arm around her back and feeling the silk of her hair. Familiarity quickly returned and they were soon entwined in an embrace as old as time. He couldn't tell where she ended and he began. He sent a silent thanks to the heavens that the two of them were together again. Then a rolling bump against his upper thigh reminded him that they were about to be three, so he sent up a thanks for that too.

They fell asleep like that. Callie awoke first, feeling badly that she'd allowed the injured Jake to fall asleep in an awkward position on the sofa. His face, highlighted by the moving screen of the television, silently grimaced and she wasn't sure how to wake him without disorienting him, so Callie leaned over him, putting an arm to each side of his head and kissed him gently, first on his forehead and then on each cheek, then his lips.

As she brushed his lips, Jake's eyes opened slowly, fraught with the pain and exhaustion of post-traumatic sleep. He saw Callie and every delicious feature on her creamy face and with a groan, part pain and part pleasure, he pulled her onto his lap. He ground against her, causing her to gasp in surprise, a swift flame of desire shooting through her core.

"Jake, are you sure you should be inviting this?" She worried that she would hurt him.

"Oh, yes, Callie. I've never wanted you more than I do right now." He nuzzled one of her breasts for emphasis and the heat pooled low in Callie's pelvis, melting her reserve.

"But I'm huge!"

"You're beautiful, voluptuous, the sexiest I've ever seen you." His eyes began to glow with passion. Callie reached for the remote and turned off the television and turned to reclaim Jake's mouth, tasting him, taunting him.

Jake rose from the couch, and after she handed him his crutches, led her to the bedroom, to their bed. They made slow, passionate love, exploring every hollow, tasting every surface, finding each point of pleasure.

Sleep claimed them long into the night, any

reservations about sharing Callie's home evaporating into satiety. Her filmy ruby maternity negligee, purchased for Jake's first night home, lay forgotten in her bureau drawer. Jake and Callie were right where they needed to be—in each other's arms, naked, replete— their love secure at last.

Jake invited Sean and Leah and V.J. over for dinner two weeks after his release from the hospital. He ordered out from his favorite French restaurant and told Callie that they were having a baby shower. Their guests did bring gifts for the baby, but the surprise was on Callie when Jake handed his crutches off to Leah and got carefully down on both knees and asked her to marry him.

Callie accepted in a flurry of tears and warm wishes from the people she loved most. She and Jake were going to be married. That wasn't, however, what would bind him to her forever. As she felt their baby pelt her ribcage, reflecting her glee, she knew their child would be the greatest evidence of the love they shared.

Epilogue

*F*elicia's prediction turned out to be prophetic. Barron Jacob Lamb was born on September the 15th. He was a strapping boy, nearly nine pounds and twenty-three inches long. Jake beamed, as proud a papa as there ever was, wandering the halls, showing off his new baby to his coworkers. Lanny rewarded him with a stout clap on the back and a cigar proclaiming 'It's a Boy'.

Jolynn and Felipa exclaimed over little Barron and brought him snuggly little outfits in blue, since everything Callie had bought was either yellow or green. Mack brought them the smallest baseball glove Callie had ever seen. They took him home to her apartment, but only temporarily since Jake's new home was due for completion in the spring. He bought out the neighbors on each side of him so that they could have free space on both sides for a fenced yard for Bob and for Barron and any other baby that might come along. Jake predicted that they would have, gasp, at least four.

Leah and Sean were six months behind Callie and Jake in adding to their family, only their addition was a litter of pups—a cross between red-coated bloodhounds and Burmese Mountain dogs. There were five squirrelly little pups and Bob beamed with pride much as Jake had. Jake and Callie agreed to take a female from the litter and Leah and Sean planned to keep one of the males. V.J., resigned that he would never find the man of his dreams, instead took a female puppy for companionship.

The other two pups went to good homes via the hospital network.

V.J. opened two more stores after the post-earthquake mess was cleaned up. He took advantage of the mass exit that often accompanied a natural disaster and snatched up the new properties for a song. He scoured the dictionary and came up with two more V.J names—*Veritable Jewels* and *Vowels Jubilee*. Callie was forced to hire an assistant—she retained full creative control, of course—and she was allowed to bring Barron along to work. He was quite fond of his playpen, preferring being in it rather than outside of it until he began to walk. He then became adept at stacking books for his mommy, toddling around with his buttery blond curls, cat-shaped green eyes, and full ruby lips, capturing the hearts of coworkers and customers alike.

Barron was eighteen months old when he toddled down the sidewalk of his parents' new home in Pacific Heights, bearing a silken pillow and two platinum rings, each studded with a flawless diamond. His parents watched his progress with pride and pure joy. They said their vows in the presence of a minister and a crowd of guests. Barron stood between them, his face turned up to his beaming parents as he babbled his approval.

Spring blossoms of fresh landscaping mingled with air laden with the smell of fresh paint and wood from their newly completed town home, which had finally been finished exactly one year past its scheduled completion. It was well worth the wait, though, for a home three stories and slightly larger than the original. They filled the home with salvaged antique wood trim, banisters, and flooring, then engaged artisans to recreate the Victorian appeal of Jake's former house. The slate blue exterior and white gingerbread trim served as a lovely backdrop for their long-anticipated wedding.

Callie often looked back on their wedding day as

the perfect expression of a love that had begun on that white sand beach. She couldn't have pictured a lovelier wedding day.

They were married just six months when Jake finally talked Callie into taking skin resurfacing treatments for the remainder of her scars. He had a colleague who specialized in cosmetic surgery and elected to resurface Callie's arms and torso with periodic dermabrasion treatments. Without surgery, her body began to transform every bit as much as her desolate heart had.

*J*ake moved back to day shifts at the hospital so he could be with Callie and Barron as much as possible outside work hours. He studied for an additional specialty in wound care, learning how to treat patients in a bariatric chamber and overseeing the first installation of such a unit at *St. Katherine's*. Leah's moms, Shirley and Eileen, donated to *St. Katherine's* the profits from the sale of their bookstore in Seattle, requesting that the new unit be named after their late son, Garrett.

They retired happily to San Diego, within driving distance of their beloved daughter, Leah, and son-in-law, Sean.

Leah and Sean, Eileen and Shirley, Jake, Callie, and Barron, V.J., and many friends and well-wishers gathered for the dedication of the *Garrett Foster-Westfield Center for Profound Healing*. Shirley made her way over to V.J. after the ceremony and introduced him to a 'friend' she and Eileen met in their new neighborhood. V.J. blushed as he talked with the former aviator and fellow book-lover. He looked at Callie helplessly from across the room and she winked and whisked her beautiful son over to ride on the shoulders of his daddy.

Callie wore a short-sleeved peasant blouse to the

occasion, marking the special event with a milestone of her own. Jake's pride in his family shone in his eyes and Callie basked in it as she gave him a solid kiss.

Barron rode high on the love of the day, secure for then and for always with his proud mommy looking on: A woman no longer scarred and lonely, but blessed in every respect.

About the Author

Kimberly Ann Freel lives in rural Washington State on a working alfalfa ranch with her husband and four children. She was recently honored as a finalist for her first two novels, *Monster White Lies* (Young Adult Fiction) and *Painted Rocks: A Novel* (Multicultural Fiction) by the **2008 Next Generation Indie Book Awards**. *Callie of the White Sand* is her third novel.

Learn more at **www.kimfreel.com**.